## "Do you, Enzo Alessandro Beresi, take Rebecca Emily Foley to be your wife?"

He looked her in the eye adoringly and without any hesitation said, "I do."

And now it was her turn.

"Do you, Rebecca Emily Foley, take Enzo Alessandro Beresi..."

She breathed in, looked Enzo straight in the eye and, in the strongest voice she could muster, loud enough for the entire congregation to clearly hear, said, "No. I. Do. Not."

Enzo's head jerked back as if she'd slapped him. A half smile froze on his tanned face, which was now drained of color. His mouth opened but nothing came out.

The only thing that had kept Rebecca together since she'd opened the package that morning was imagining this moment and inflicting an iota of the pain and humiliation racking her on him. There was none of the satisfaction she'd longed for. The speech she'd prepared in her head died in her choked throat.

Unable to look at him a second longer, she wrenched her hands from his and walked back down the aisle, leaving a stunned silence in her wake.

**Michelle Smart**'s love affair with books started when she was a baby and would cuddle them in her cot. A voracious reader of all genres, she found her love of romance established when she stumbled across her first Harlequin book at the age of twelve. She's been reading them—and writing them—ever since. Michelle lives in Northamptonshire, England, with her husband and two young Smarties.

### Books by Michelle Smart

#### Harlequin Presents

*Stranded with Her Greek Husband*
*Claiming His Baby at the Altar*

#### A Billion-Dollar Revenge

*Bound by the Italian's "I Do"*

#### Scandalous Royal Weddings

*Crowning His Kidnapped Princess*
*Pregnant Innocent Behind the Veil*
*Rules of Their Royal Wedding Night*

Visit the Author Profile page
at Harlequin.com for more titles.

# *Michelle Smart*

—

## INNOCENT'S WEDDING DAY WITH THE ITALIAN

HARLEQUIN
PRESENTS

**HARLEQUIN®**
**PRESENTS™**

Recycling programs
for this product may
not exist in your area.

ISBN-13: 978-1-335-59182-1

Innocent's Wedding Day with the Italian

Harlequin Enterprises ULC
22 Adelaide St. West, 41st Floor
Toronto, Ontario M5H 4E3, Canada
www.Harlequin.com

Printed in U.S.A.

# INNOCENT'S WEDDING
# DAY WITH THE ITALIAN

For Mitchell. May the world always be this exciting and loving for you xxx

# CHAPTER ONE

THE STRETCH LIMOUSINE was greeted in the piazza by dozens of cameras flashing manically. Since the announcement of her engagement, Rebecca Foley had avoided cameras like the plague. She'd known it would be impossible to avoid them today, the day of the wedding of the century. Italy's premier bachelor was about to get hitched, and she was the lucky lady he was pledging his life to.

While waiting for the driver to open her door, Rebecca looked at the empty space beside her where her father should be. This car she was about to be helped out of should be *his* car, the 1960s battered classic he'd been so proud of getting for a steal, as he'd called it, the year she'd set off for university. Each visit home had seen him proudly showing off all his painstakingly slow improvements.

He'd died with the renovations unfinished. Leaving the car locked in a storage facility had been the biggest wrench for Rebecca when she'd made her move to Italy, harder than leaving the only real home she'd ever known.

She fisted her hands and clenched her teeth at the pang that ripped through her. Four years since the death of her parents and today the pain of missing them was as sharp as it had been in those terrible dark days. She'd never needed them more than she did right now.

The door opened.

The driver held his hand out for her.

It wasn't just the paparazzi capturing the bride's arrival outside the domed cathedral but hundreds of well-wishers too, all lining the cordons Enzo had paid the authorities to erect. Having oodles of money meant the barriers normal people faced could be circumvented. It was the greasing of his money that allowed the opulent car transporting her onto the public square vehicles were usually forbidden from entering.

Taking a deep breath, Rebecca straightened her back, fixed a smile to her face, put one foot in front of the other and prayed not to trip over her dress. Shouts of encouragement followed her into the famous Florentine cathedral.

She'd imagined this moment for so long. The wedding had taken months of planning by a highly specialised team. She'd envisaged Enzo's expression when he saw her in the fairy-tale dress of her dreams and, when he turned at the far end of the aisle to face her, it didn't disappoint. Every step closer to him brought that expression into clearer focus and brought him into clearer focus too.

Enzo Beresi. Self-made billionaire. A six-foot-two hunk of pure muscle injected with testosterone. An Italian success story. Dark brown hair worn stylishly messy. Always immaculate and dapperly dressed. The kind of man women salivated for and men wished they could be. Easy-going to a fault. Charming. Even-tempered. Ethical. Renowned for his charitable works. A liar.

Throughout their whirlwind five-month romance in which he'd proposed four weeks after their first date, Rebecca had constantly asked herself *why me*? Why had Enzo Beresi set his sights on her, a twenty-four-year-old primary schoolteacher, when he had the pick of the world's most eligible women? He could have had *anyone*. But he had chosen her. He had swept her off her feet. And Rebecca had fallen head over heels in love with him.

As she neared the altar, her father's sister, Rebecca's closest living relative, the woman who'd done so much to help her through the trauma of losing both her parents within three days of each other, appeared in her eyeline. She was sat in the space usually reserved for the mother of the bride.

Rebecca blurred her aunt out before the pain of the loss of her parents and the loss of her future grew too big to endure.

She reached Enzo.

His incredible body clothed in a dark grey tuxedo with a swallowtail jacket and dusky pink cravat, his translucent brown eyes sparkled. He mouthed the cliché that must come from every groom's lips. 'You look beautiful.'

He was so good. So believable. That gorgeous, chiselled face with its generous mouth and aquiline nose composed itself into an expression of adoration as he took her hand and drew her to him.

It sickened her that she could still react

with such violent intensity to his touch. Sickened her that she could still want the man who'd never wanted her.

His insistence that they wait for their wedding night to consummate their marriage had not been the romantic gesture she'd reluctantly gone along with.

It had all been a set-up.

He'd never truly wanted her. He'd only wanted what marrying her could bring him.

At least she now had the answer to the *why me?* question.

Hands entwined, they turned to the priest. The five hundred–strong congregation filled with the rich, the powerful and the beautiful rose as one. The wedding service began.

All the months of planning and Rebecca had envisaged that the service itself would drag, that she'd be mentally urging the priest to get a move on and get to the good bit. She'd practiced her Italian until she could say her vows faultlessly. Sure, it was only two words—*I do*—but she'd wanted her accent to be perfect.

Now that she was living it, she found herself wishing the order of service to have the brakes applied. The closer they got to the moment, the quicker time passed and the more her heart threatened to burst from her ribs.

The priest got to the meat of it all.

They faced each other and clasped hands.

'Do you, Enzo Alessandro Beresi, take Rebecca Emily Foley to be your wife…?'

She was going to be sick.

He looked her in the eye adoringly and without any hesitation said, 'I do.'

And now it was her turn.

'Do you, Rebecca Emily Foley, take Enzo Alessandro Beresi…?'

She breathed in, looked Enzo straight in the eye and, in the strongest voice she could muster, loud enough for the entire congregation to clearly hear, said, 'No. I. Do. Not.'

Enzo's head jerked back as if she'd slapped him. The half smile froze on the tanned face that drained of colour. His mouth opened but nothing came out.

The only thing that had kept Rebecca together since she'd opened the package earlier that day was imagining this moment and inflicting an iota of the pain and humiliation racking her on him. Only there was none of the satisfaction she'd longed for. The speech she'd prepared in her head died in her choked throat.

Unable to look at him a second longer, she wrenched her hands from his and walked back down the aisle leaving a stunned silence in her wake.

It was only when Rebecca stepped outside onto the cathedral steps and into the Florentine heat that the magnitude of it all hit her.

Several hours ago, minutes before the hair stylist had arrived, the anonymous package had been delivered to the hotel with her name, suite number and *Urgent* written clearly on it, and the cloud of happiness she'd been living in had been torn apart. And now she felt it in the core of her being, an agony ripping through her soul.

She staggered down the steps. Suddenly, the amassed paparazzi, reporters and well-wishers, all busy chatting amongst themselves while they waited for the service to finish, noticed the bride had left her own wedding twenty minutes early. Before they could scramble into position, Rebecca hitched up the skirt of her silk and lace dress and set off over the piazza at a run, past the limousine waiting to transport the happy couple to the reception, past the ancient fountain which crowds of people were congregated around, oblivious to the gawps, deaf to the calls of concern. She had no destination in mind, just an overwhelming need to flee as far as it was possible to get from the man who'd ripped her heart in two. She would have run until the heels of her shoes had worn to nothing if she hadn't caught a heel in a cobble and gone sprawling like a child, landing palms down and coming within an inch of smashing her face on the ancient ground.

*'Signorina?'*

In a flash, a group of adolescent males whiling their day away admiring each other's Vespas and generally doing their best T-bird impressions, came to her aid.

A cloud of cheap aftershave enveloped her as she was solicitously helped back to her feet, her hands examined for injuries and the rips in the lace of her two-hundred-thousand-euro dress clucked over. She tried to say thank you as she wiped away the tears streaming down her face but her throat was still too choked. She did manage a form of laughter when shaking her head at a cigarette.

Was that what she'd come to? A damsel in such distress it seemed reasonable to offer her a cigarette?

In the distance behind her came a shout, rapidly followed by more shouts. Those congregating inside and outside the cathedral were on the move. From the hollers, she guessed they'd spotted her. Her fairy-tale white wedding dress hardly made her inconspicuous.

She nodded at the row of Vespas and, her Italian deserting her, asked in English, 'Can I have a lift please?'

Only one face didn't respond with a blank look. 'Where you want to go, lady?'

She gave the name of the tree-lined avenue Enzo's villa was located. Six sets of eyes widened. And no wonder. It was one of the most exclusive areas of Florence. 'Please?' she beseeched. *'Per favore?'*

Looking over her shoulder at the growing crowd heading their way and catching her urgent desperation, the young men sprang into action. Before she knew it, Rebecca was on a Vespa, the skirt of her dress tucked as well as it could be between her legs, clinging tightly to a skinny young man she doubted needed to shave regularly, and then they were off. With the rest of his gang coming along for the ride, her saviour zipped through the traffic. The journey should have taken a mini-

mum of twenty minutes but by treating the
rules of the road as an old-fashioned inconvenience and tooting his horn at any pedes-
trian stupid enough to attempt to cross in
front of them, they soon left the bustle of the
city proper, and fifteen minutes after they
set out, her saviour came to a stop outside
Enzo's electric gate.

She jumped off the Vespa and punched
the code to open it. 'Can you take me to the
airport?' she asked as the gate opened. 'I'll
pay.' She had cash in her purse.

Her saviour's mouth, open in stunned awe
at the sprawling whitewashed villa with its
terracotta roofs, snapped shut. He smiled.
'Okay, lady.'

'Five minutes.' She held up her still-bleed-
ing palm with fingers and thumb stretched
out to stress the point, and ran up the drive to
the front door. Before she reached it, Frank,
Enzo's uber-professional butler, shot out of
his adjoining quarters.

'What has happened?' he asked in care-
ful English. Barely a day ago he'd carried
her overnight bags and wedding dress to the
car waiting to take her to the hotel she would
spend her final night as a single lady in, and
wished her the happiest of wedding days.

Fearing she would start crying again, Rebecca shook her head.

Concern writ all over his face, he opened the door for her.

Inside, she wasted no time. Kicking off her white shoes, she hurried through the vast ornate reception room, through the arch that led to the east wing, and ran over the terracotta-floored corridor to the cinema room. The walls were lined with original prints of advertisements for Hollywood movies from the fifties and sixties. She went straight to the one with a beautiful blonde flanked by two men in swimming trunks and removed it. She remembered how she'd laughed when Enzo had shown her the safe. Remembered too, the grin on his face when he'd put her passport in it a week ago. She'd thought it a grin of happiness that she'd finally moved in with him, even if they were sticking to separate bedrooms, at his insistence, until the wedding. If only she'd known it was because she was one step closer to giving him what he really wanted. Which wasn't her. It had never been her, and as she placed her eye to the retina scanner, memories of the day they'd met five months ago filtered like a reel in her mind.

Her aunt's fiftieth birthday lunch at a beautiful country hotel. The weather as cold and grey as the cloud that had cloaked Rebecca for three and a half years. Her dismay when she left the lunch party to find her car had a flat tyre. Hauling the spare out of the boot. Wrestling with the wheel nuts. The gorgeous man with the heartbreaking dimpled smile and the most amazing translucent brown eyes that danced with merriment, who'd jumped out of the back of a car worth more than her house and offered his help. *Insisted.*

The memories solidified as she remembered how he'd removed his long, dark brown overcoat and the jacket of a suit that clearly cost more than her entire wardrobe and handed them to her to hold for him. They'd carried the most amazing, woody scent. He'd then rolled his sleeves up and sank onto the cold, wet ground. Throughout his expert tyre change he'd kept up a steady stream of talk, all in the most gorgeous deep, velvet voice and with the most fantastic accent her ears had ever heard. When he'd finished, Rebecca had been mortified to find his expensive trousers and shirt were stained with dirt and grease.

'You must send me the dry cleaning bill,'

she'd insisted through chattering teeth when she passed his suit jacket back to him. 'It's the least I can do.'

He'd slipped his arms into it, his eyes gleaming. 'Or,' he'd said, 'you can join me in the hotel bar and we can defrost over a hot drink by the fire.'

She could still feel echoes of the jolt of excitement that had shot through her.

Even though she'd already checked his ring finger, something she had never done before, she'd handed his overcoat to him unable to stop her gaze from dipping again to his bare left hand. 'How is that repayment?'

'The associate I am meeting is running late and so I am at a loose end for the next hour. If you keep me company, I will be less likely to die of boredom.'

She'd grinned at his drollness.

IIis dimples had reappeared. 'You will be doing me a favour. One drink and we will be even.'

Her smile at this declaration was so wide that for the first time in over three and a half years, Rebecca had felt the muscles of her cheeks working. 'One drink. And I'm paying.'

He'd frowned and tutted. 'A gentleman never lets a lady pay.'

She'd raised her eyebrows in her best school-teacher fashion. 'Did the turn of the twenty-first century pass you by?'

Amusement had danced between them and then they'd both started laughing, and to remember how it had been and the connection she'd felt with him right from the start and know it had all been staged, that he'd punctured her tyre himself...

The green light of the safe flashed and blinded the memories away. The reinforced door swung open.

Her heart wrenched to see her passport exactly where he'd put it, nestled on top of his.

Swallowing back another roll of nausea, Rebecca snatched hers up, pushed the safe's door shut, then raced back into the corridor, ran up the closest stairs two at a time, and hurtled to the bedroom she'd used since her first visit to the villa all those months ago.

How long did she have, she wondered, her mind racing as to where Enzo could be. Would he think to look for her here? Or would he go straight to the hotel she'd stayed the night at and which they and their guests were supposed to head to for the evening celebrations?

Grabbing her handbag, she dropped her passport into it next to her purse. Her phone was at the hotel but that couldn't be helped. She had enough cash to get to the airport and enough money in her bank account to get herself home.

About to leave the room, she caught sight of her appearance in the full-length mirror and almost crumbled. Her perfectly made-up oval face, perfect because it had been done by a professional makeup artist, was a mascara-streaked mess. Her large brown eyes were red-rimmed, her too-wide mouth pulled in tightly to stop the scream of anguish fighting to escape from it. The artful up-do the celebrity stylist had spent so long working on was gone, her honey blonde hair and ripped dress now giving her the look of someone who'd been dragged through a gooseberry bush backwards. Swallowing back the scream with all the strength her throat could muster, Rebecca yanked the clip holding what remained of the original do together. She was already out of the door before the rest of her hair fell to her shoulders.

As she hitched up the skirt of her ruined fairy-tale dress and flew back to the stairs and down to the ground floor, she imagined the shops at the airport. She'd be able to buy clothes to change into…

She skidded to a halt, the scream leaving her throat before her senses properly registered the man standing guard at the front door.

Rebecca's heart, already pounding from the exertion of tearing around the villa, slammed hard into her ribs.

Towering over her, Enzo's chiselled jaw was clenched. The colour had returned to his tanned olive skin but the designer messiness of his hair had lost the designer quality to it. The dusky pink cravat that had graced his strong neck in the cathedral had gone, the top buttons of his white shirt undone.

'Get out of my way,' she whispered, finding her voice.

His answer was to fold his arms across his broad chest.

It made her broken heart splinter that bit more to understand she must be seeing the real Enzo Beresi for the first time.

'I said get out of my way.'

His folded arms tightened, the muscles visibly flexing. His nostrils flared. 'No.'

A swell of rage punched through her. Launching herself at him, she pushed at him, trying to shove him away from the door. 'Get out of my way!' she shouted.

But he was too big, too muscular, too *sub-*

*stantial*. With an agility no man his size should possess, he held her arms to her sides and then twisted her around and pinned her to him so her back was pressed tight against his solid chest, his muscular arm trapping her to him.

'Stop that,' he snarled when she started kicking back at him and the heel of her bare foot made contact with his shin.

'Let me go!'

'When you are calm.' His breath hot in her hair, his velvet, accented voice calmed as if to display what he required of her. 'There is nowhere for you to run. I have sent your Vespa boys away.'

'Then I'll get a taxi.'

'And go where? The airport?'

'I want to go *home*.'

'You *are* home.'

'No.' She shook her head. Salt water spilled down her cheeks to remember the joy that had consumed her to imagine filling this beautiful villa with Enzo's babies and the blissfully happy life they would have together. 'No.'

'Why did you do it?' he asked, not loosening his hold around her. 'Tell me, Rebecca. Tell me why you did it.'

'Why do you *think*? And if you don't let

me go this second I'm going to scream loud enough for the whole of Florence to hear.'

He spun her round with the same speed and agility he'd pinned her to him. Large hands gripping her shoulders, rage contorted the handsome features bearing down on hers. 'You dare play the injured party when you were planning to take your passport and run away from me without a word of explanation or goodbye? When you have humiliated me in front of the whole damn world? I had to steal a Vespa to get here before you could run. Tell me why you did that to me. You owe me that much.'

'I don't owe you anything,' she cried, pushing at his chest. 'I know, damn you. I know exactly why you were marrying me. It was all a set-up!'

For the second time in less than an hour the colour drained from Enzo's face. He staggered, groping behind him for the door which he propped himself up against. His throat moved before he whispered, 'Rebecca…'

'Don't! I don't want to hear your lies. I know everything. *Everything*. You never loved me or wanted me. The only thing you wanted was my inheritance.'

# CHAPTER TWO

WATCHING ENZO COMPOSE himself was something that in ordinary circumstances Rebecca would marvel at, was something she *had* marvelled at. Never had she been in greater awe at this ability than the few times he'd come close to losing his control and making love to her as she'd pleaded for him to do. His breaths would be hot and heavy, his skin fevered, his arousal solid and visible through the clothes he always kept on, but always he would pull himself back. One long, deep breath through his nose and the passion that had blazed from his eyes would vanish and his composure would be assured.

At least she knew now how he'd been able to manage that side of things so well. While she'd been sitting there physically aching with need for him, it had been no real effort on his part to disengage his brain from his body's responses. His responses to her had been nothing but an automatic reaction. She could have been any reasonably attractive woman.

Back straight, his light brown eyes locked on hers. 'How did you find out?'

She laughed through the tears. 'Is that the first thing you think to ask? All you care about?'

'I ask because it's important.'

'A package marked urgent was delivered by a woman to the hotel reception for me. I don't know or care who the woman was.'

A swathe of emotions flickered over his darkening features. 'It was a copy of your grandfather's will?'

Another swell of rage pulsed through her from deep in her stomach all the way to the tips of her fingers and toes.

Once, over the course of a meal, Rebecca had mentioned that she'd never met her mother's parents because of an estrangement that had occurred before she was born. Only now did she make the link to his brief show of sympathy and then an abrupt changing of the subject to it being because it was something he already knew. Enzo knew her past better than she did.

He knew it because he'd been her grandfather's business partner and the man her grandfather had trusted enough to appoint as executor to his will.

That meant Enzo must have known about her parents too. The evening Rebecca had cuddled into him with her head on his chest and relayed how her dad had suffered a fatal heart attack only three days after her mother's death from blood cancer, a blow that had rocked the foundations of her world, a grief she'd never believed she would recover from, Enzo had stroked her back and murmured words of comfort and he'd *already known*.

'How could you do this to me?' Her anger was such that to hear the pain resonate in her voice only added fresh anguish, because it meant *he* could hear it too. 'All this time. All those lies. You told me you loved me and all you ever wanted was his business. Now let me go. It hurts to even look at you.'

Not an ounce of remorse flickered on his set features. *Nothing* flickered. His self-control was too strong. 'Remember all the press covering our wedding? They are already outside the gates. Leave now and they will eat you alive.'

'As if you care what happens to me.'

'I care.'

'Don't *lie*,' she screamed, losing control again and hurtling her handbag across the room. It hit an eighteenth-century eighteen-inch marble statue, knocking it off its plinth and sending it to the floor where it shattered with an ear-piercing shriek. The way Rebecca felt, she could make her way through the entire villa and systematically destroy every object he held dear, shatter it all into the same fragments Enzo had shattered her heart into. 'Every word ever exchanged between us has been a lie.'

Chiselled jaw clenched, he shook his head. 'No.'

'Another lie! I gave up everything for you and it was all a lie. You wanted an explanation as to why I humiliated you in the cathedral and now you've heard it. I don't want to spend another second in your company so get out of my way and let me leave. I never want to see you again.'

The clear brown eyes she'd gazed into with her heart filled with such love and hope held hers without expression before closing. His throat moved and his chest rose slowly as if he were trying to control emotions she now knew he didn't possess. And then he walked away from the door and crunched over the shards and splinters of marble to pick up her bag and hold it out to her.

Without a word, she plucked it from his hand and headed out of the door.

The moment her bare feet touched the marble steps, a cacophony of noise and light that rivalled the beaming sun engulfed her. Straight ahead, at the end of the driveway, behind the high electric gates, the press and paparazzi who'd lined the cordons outside the cathedral stood packed and jostling for position. The scramble of questions being shouted at her came close to being drowned out by the helicopter swooping in her direction overhead.

She stood there for the longest time, staring at the pack who, with one comment from her, had the power to bring Enzo Beresi down. His philanthropic, good-guy persona would be destroyed with just eight words.

*He was marrying me to steal my inheritance.*

The swelling of pain and rage shifted and hardened, and injected her spine with steel. She walked slowly towards the pack, barely blinking as the camera flashes grew stronger.

*He was marrying me to steal my inheritance.*

And then she stopped.

Rebecca knew what he'd done. She knew why he'd done it. What she didn't know was how.

She spun back to the villa.

The reception room was empty of life. Treading her way carefully around the wreckage of the marble statue, she found Enzo at the bar at the far end of the sprawling double-height living room that looked out over the vast, manicured grounds she'd imagined their children playing in. He was pouring himself a drink, his back to her.

The impulse to turn back around and leave like she'd intended was strong but she fought it. She deserved answers. She *needed* answers.

'I've changed my mind.'

Her words flew across the huge room and landed on him like an electric pulse, making his head snap back.

'I'm still leaving but first, you owe me answers,' she said stonily. 'I'm going to get changed and pack my things. While I'm doing that, you can pour me a gin and tonic and arrange for a car to collect me. When I come back down, we will have one last drink together and you will explain what it is you hate so much about me that you thought I deserved to be treated with such cruelty.'

Other than the movement of one shoulder, he didn't react to her stony words or turn around to face her, and for that she was glad. It meant he didn't see the tear trickle down her cheek. Wiping it away, she went back up to her room.

It had taken three women over an hour to sew Rebecca into her wedding dress. Using her nail scissors, she ripped her way out of it in seconds. Then she stripped off her underwear and stood before her full-length mirror.

What was it about her body that had repelled him into not consummating their relationship, she wondered miserably. She remembered the moment she'd told Enzo that she was a virgin. It was after their third date. He'd invited her back to his London apartment. He'd been so smooth. So suave. So flipping gorgeous. She'd already been smitten by that point. She'd accepted his invitation with butterflies like she'd never imagined existed loose in her belly, butterflies that had strengthened as they'd taken his private elevator to his penthouse. Then, when she'd crossed the threshold into an apartment more palatial than her wildest conjuring and he'd pressed her against a wall and started kissing her with such fervent desire, she'd responded with a heat so wanton and *vital* that she'd blurted out her virgin state before things went too far and she forgot to tell him later on.

He'd backed right off.

At the time, she'd taken him at face value, that her being a virgin meant they shouldn't rush things. Once she'd accepted his proposal his next excuse had been that he wanted their wedding night to be the most special night of both their lives. She'd taken that at face value too, had been *thrilled* at the romantic notion behind it, even if his absolute refusal to budge from it had driven her steadily insane.

'Good things come to those who wait, *cara*,' he'd often said with a cheeky wink that had always melted her insides. When she'd questioned why he'd never felt the need to wait for the legion of women who'd come before her, he'd answered with a simple, 'They meant nothing to me, not when compared to how I feel about you.'

That morning, she'd woken buzzing with excitement at marrying him and practically giddy with anticipation that, finally, they would make love, had even done an internet search to learn the minimum acceptable time to leave your own wedding reception so you could slope off to bed with your new husband. That was before the package had been delivered and her heart smashed into smithereens of course.

Enzo had used her virginity as the excuse he needed not to bed her, and now she studied her naked body and naked face and wondered what he'd found so repulsive about them that he'd grabbed the first excuse that had come along to back off from having to make love to her. She knew she was a little on the skinny side but she couldn't help that. And neither could she help her small breasts. Both were an inheritance from her mum. Not that he'd seen her breasts or the dark pink nipples that topped them. He'd felt them though. He'd even remembered to fake a groan before removing his hand from under her top. He couldn't be repulsed by her pubic hair because he hadn't seen that either, or even felt it. His hands had never roamed her skin below the waist. Gropes of her backside didn't count.

She supposed he would have forced himself to make love to her and consummate the marriage. Yes, he'd have wanted the con-summation done as quickly as possible. He wouldn't have risked an annulment.

Even Enzo's impatience to marry her as soon as was humanly possible had been a lie. The biggest lie of all.

Unable to stare at herself a moment longer, she stood beneath the shower and, as the hot water sprayed over her body, tried her hard-est to scrub the day and all of Enzo's lies off her skin.

Clean and dry, dressed in faded jeans and a loose black V-necked top with elbow-length sleeves, what she could cram of her clothes packed in one of the carry-on cases Enzo had bought for her first visit to Florence, Rebecca left her room for the last time, leaving behind the array of designer clothing rammed in her dressing room, all of which he'd bought for her. On her dressing table amidst the array of perfumes he'd also bought her, sat her en-gagement ring.

She was glad she was doing it this way rather than running away as had been her instinct. It was cleaner like this.

She would force Enzo to explain himself

and then she would leave properly, with her head held high and her dignity intact.

She had the rest of her life to fix her shattered heart.

The marble fragments had already been cleaned away. Rebccca put her case by the front door. Peering through a window, she saw a large black car with blacked-out windows parked at the front. Her getaway car. She was quite sure the driver would run over the marauding press if necessary.

Ankle boots placed ready by her case, she padded her way back to the living area.

Her gin and tonic was waiting for her on a small round glass table but Enzo had disappeared.

Taking a deep breath, she had a long drink of it and curled up on her favourite squishy round chair.

The composure she'd worked so hard to find almost shattered in sympathy with her heart at his appearance.

From the dampness of his hair, he'd showered too. His wedding suit had been replaced with a pair of faded jeans, and a V-necked black T-shirt. Like hers, his feet were bare.

A day ago, it would have sent a thrill racing through her that they had independently mimicked each other's clothing. Now it made her stomach clench painfully.

Gripping tightly to her glass to stop the tremors in her hands betraying her, she had another long drink. How could he have paid such attention that he knew exactly how she liked her gin and tonic, even down to her preferred number of ice cubes?

She was forgetting his big brain, she reminded herself. How else could a thirty-three-year-old be a self-made billionaire without an oversized brain? And smarts. He had that in abundance too. The kind of smarts that came from a different part of the brain to mere cleverness. It was a combination that had fascinated her from their first real conversation in the hotel bar on that cold winter day. She remembered it so clearly, right down to the crackle of the log fire they'd sat beside nursing their hot drinks.

Shy with strangers—unless they were small children—Enzo's open, gregarious nature and beautiful velvety voice had put Rebecca at an ease she'd never felt before. She could have listened to him speak for hours and she only realised she'd been watching the time pass with increasing trepidation when he'd asked if he could see her again and her delight and relief had bloomed like a flower under the bright rising sun.

But even then, even at that very first meet, had been the nagging question: *Why me?* This street-smart, clever, suave, gorgeous, rich man every woman in the hotel bar kept side-eying liked *her*? He wanted to see *her* again?

Deep down she'd known all along that it was too good to be true. If only she'd listened to that incredulous nagging voice all those months ago...

Enzo nodded at her glass.

She nodded back, finished her drink, put the glass on the table and pushed it towards him.

He stepped closer to take it. The crisp clean scent of freshly showered Enzo hit her. It was a scent that had greeted her so many times these last five months and which never failed to make her want to throw herself at him. Resisting that temptation since moving in had become a game, but it was no game now, and she curled deeper into the sofa and wrapped her arms around her calves.

Once he'd made them both another drink and warily placed her glass back on the table—she imagined the wariness came from him wondering if she was going to throw it at him—he sat on the edge of the two-seater sofa closest to hers, both feet on the floor, had a sip of his Scotch and then put his tumbler and a half-full bottle of Scotch on the glass table beside his seat.

Rebecca blinked away the memory created just four days ago when she'd laughingly said they would have to change the living room drinks tables when they had children. Glass tables and small children were a combination she'd thought best not tested. He'd laughed, and then turned his face away as if his mind had been captured by something else. Used to that strange quirk of his whenever she idly contemplated their future, she hadn't thought anything more about it, but now she knew the truth. He'd turned his face away so she wouldn't see the mockery behind the laughter.

She breathed in deeply, watching as he clasped his hands together and placed them on his lap.

His chest rose slowly before he looked at her and said, 'Rebecca, I know it is hard for you to believe but I never lied about my feelings for you.'

'Save your breath,' she dismissed. 'I'm not marrying you. My grandfather's business shares will never be yours.'

'I don't care about the shares.'

Genuinely amused at the blatancy of his lie, she laughed, then laughed harder to see him flinch. 'Does lying come to you as naturally as breathing? Don't answer that,' she added when he opened his mouth. 'I'll only assume it's another lie.'

'Rebecca...'

'And stop saying my name before you taint it for good.' He was the only one to call her Rebecca. To her parents she'd been Becs. To the rest of her family, friends, colleagues and distant acquaintances she was Becky. *Everyone* shortened it. Everyone except Enzo. She'd adored the way her full name rolled off his tongue. To hear it roll off his tongue now hurt immeasurably.

His lips clamped together and formed a straight line, the bones of his jaw virtually breaking the skin.

She'd bet no one had spoken to him like this in a decade. Maybe that was part of the reason he was an unconscionable bastard. He should have known better than to mess with a primary schoolteacher. They were pros when it came to dealing with liars, even if the liars were generally three and a half feet high and struggled to do their own shoelaces up. She'd never imagined those lying traits could continue so long into adulthood.

She shifted in her seat, reached for her drink, crossed her legs and faced him properly. Forced herself to look at him properly. Dispassionately.

'Here's how we're going to play it,' she said in her best teacher's voice. 'I'm going to ask you questions and you're going to answer them, clearly and concisely. Stick to the facts. Do not attempt to justify yourself unless I ask. If you have to think before you answer I will assume you're lying. Do not speak to me of *feelings* or *love*, and don't ask what I'm going to do about my share of the business but keep in mind that the way I'm feeling about you right now, I'm quite capable of taking advice as to how best to destroy the whole business with it.'

It had only dawned on Rebecca since taking her shower the power she held. At midnight she turned twenty-five and so would inherit half of her grandfather's business, whatever that was, although she supposed the clue was in the name, 'Claflin Diamonds'.

She didn't have to suppose that this was a business Enzo very much wanted all for himself. As if he didn't have enough, what with the multiple businesses he owned outright and all the others he invested in. The business that had made him famous though, was his chain of high-end Beresi jewellery stores, all of which stocked bespoke, exquisitely made and ethically sourced jewellery enthusiastically embraced by the rich and famous. She would love to hear what his investors and customers thought about the ethics of him marrying someone for their inheritance.

'My advice would be not to add any fuel to my anger. All I want from you is some honesty…' She came close to choking. 'If you're even capable of it.'

# CHAPTER THREE

FEATURES SET SO hard they could be carved from the same marble as the statue Rebecca had destroyed, Enzo slowly inclined his handsome face. 'Where would you like me to start?'

*I want you to start by telling me what I ever did to you that you could take my heart and use it as your personal plaything, you cruel bastard*, she wanted to scream.

But she would not scream. She would not show emotions. Not any more. She would maintain this dispassionate front until she had all the answers she needed and then walk out of his life for good.

'At the beginning. When did you go into business with my grandfather?'

'Thirteen years ago.'

She blinked in surprise. Their partnership went much further back than she'd imagined. 'How did it come about?'

'Do you remember me telling you how my first jewellery shop was a learning curve for me?'

She thought of their second date when he'd self-deprecatingly laughed as he'd explained how his business had almost ended before it had begun.

'I was naive and expected instant success but to compete with the big boys, I needed a unique selling point.'

'Man-made diamonds,' she supplied in a whisper, the penny starting to drop as she remembered Enzo saying how he'd figured the growing movement for ethically sourced products had meant an opening for ethically sourced diamonds.

'*Sì*,' he agreed tautly. 'Man-made diamonds. Your grandfather was a visionary who'd seen long before me that there would be a market for them, and invested heavily in it. But he was ahead of his time. When I came along, he was in major financial difficulties.'

The dropping penny landed in Rebecca's brain with a loud clang. The diamonds used in the jewellery Enzo's stores sold came from a laboratory. The technique used made their purity, which Beresi was famous for, indistinguishable from naturally occurring ones.

'You invested in Claflin Diamonds.'

'Yes. I bought fifty per cent of it.'

Thinking hard, she narrowed her eyes. 'How could you afford that? You could only have been twenty then…unless you were lying when you told me you didn't hit the big time until you were twenty-five.'

'No lie,' he said steadily. 'The diamonds from the laboratory played a big part in my success. The biggest part. A prominent company offered to buy the whole business from him. If he'd taken their offer, all his debts would have been paid and he'd have had cash left over to live comfortably for the rest of his life. Instead of taking it, he took a leap of faith with me and sold me the shares at a cut price. The price was enough to get him off the hook with his creditors but that was it. I paid for my half with what was left of my father's inheritance and took a personal loan for the rest.'

Rebecca would not let the mention of Enzo's father play on her heartstrings. His father had died at the age of twenty-eight when Enzo was six from a brain aneurysm, leaving an insurance policy for his son to inherit when he turned eighteen. She distinctly remembered Enzo telling her he'd used that inheritance to pay for the lease and stock of his first store. He'd made it sound as if the entire inheritance had been swallowed up by that first store. Another lie.

'And now you want all of Claflin Diamonds for yourself.'

He gave no reaction to her contempt. 'Your grandfather founded it but it belonged to both of us equally. We both made it what it is today and reaped the rewards. Without that partnership, your grandfather would have been made bankrupt and there would be no Beresi. It was agreed that when he died—and your grandfather knew he was dying—that his shares would pass to me.'

That threw her off course. 'He knew he was dying?'

His shoulders rose heavily. '*Sì*. He was diagnosed with stage four pancreatic cancer last October. Believe me, it came as a shock to us both. In all the years we'd been partners, his health had always been excellent. Your grandfather was sixty-eight but until the cancer he had the energy of a man my own age.'

Rebecca couldn't explain why this made her heart pang. She'd never met the grandfather who'd disowned her mother for marrying a man he'd deemed beneath her. His first ever contact with her had come a few weeks after her parents' deaths, a letter of condolence in which he'd asked to meet her. She'd replied with a terse, 'No thank you.' Despite her refusal, he'd taken to sending her birthday and Christmas cards with cheques enclosed. She'd returned them all, including the cheques. Just to imagine cashing them made her feel sick.

Unsure why tears were welling behind her eyes, she forced the conversation back to what really mattered at this moment. 'Okay, so he promised you his share of the business but instead of doing that, he made it conditional that you had to marry me to get it.'

And that's why it had all been one big fat lie.

Under the terms of her grandfather's will, Enzo only received the shares if he married Rebecca. If he failed to marry her before she turned twenty-five, then the shares—half of Claflin Diamonds—automatically became hers.

Rebecca turned twenty-five in approximately five hours.

'That condition my grandfather put into his will was unconscionable,' she stated into the silence. 'I don't see how any judge would have allowed it to stand.'

Enzo drained his Scotch with a grimace. 'If I'd contested it, litigation could have dragged on for years. We're talking different jurisdictions too, and there was no guarantee I would win.'

She shrugged. 'You could have waited until my birthday and just bought the shares off me. It wasn't as if you had to wait for long and you must have known I wouldn't want anything to do with the business. I'm a primary schoolteacher for cripes sake!' *Was* a primary schoolteacher, she corrected herself. She'd quit her job at the end of the summer term, which was also the end of the school year, nine days ago.

To think she'd believed Enzo had encouraged her to quit before the school year ended because he couldn't wait to make her his wife when all along he'd been working on a deadline to stop her grandfather's shares slipping out of his hands and into hers. That deadline had been her birthday.

For the first time since their conversation started, she spotted a flash of anger on the too-handsome features. 'Do you not think I went through every scenario and eventuality before settling on this path?'

'Let me throw this out there—it's a radical idea, I know—but did it ever occur to you to just be honest with me and explain the situation?'

'For about thirty seconds.'

'That long?' she mocked.

'I had no way of knowing how you would react. Without Claflin Diamonds there would be no Beresi. I was not prepared to risk losing control of it to someone who taught small children for a living and knew nothing of business. If it wasn't for my investment and the partnership we formed, there wouldn't be a business and your grandfather would have been buried in a cardboard box.'

'You went to his funeral? I didn't even know he was dead until this morning.' And she couldn't understand why his death made her feel *anything*. Ray Claflin was nothing but a malevolent name to her.

'Your grandfather arranged his own funeral before he died,' Enzo said tightly. 'He forbade me from telling you about his condition or notifying you of his death. I was the only mourner. He did not want anyone else to attend. By the end of his life he was a man haunted by many demons.'

'Whatever demons he had, I'm sure he deserved them.' Rebecca could not comprehend how a parent could disown their own child for the crime of falling in love.

Aware she was derailing herself from her interrogation, she looked back at Enzo, battling to keep her features stony. 'Why didn't you tell me about the inheritance when he died? You were his executor.'

Having been appointed executor in her parents' wills meant Rebecca knew more about the role than she could ever have wanted. She'd been meticulous about her duties, not because she was a meticulous person—she wasn't—but because it was a distraction from a grief that had made it hard to breathe.

She'd only learned to breathe properly again when a tall, dark, gorgeous Italian had swooped into her life.

Fighting hard to keep the tempest brewing inside her quelled, she added, 'You had a legal duty to tell me of my inheritance.'

The business shares were only a part of it. Rebecca inherited everything else from her grandfather outright. She had no idea what that everything else was worth, and nor did she care. She didn't want any of it… Apart from the Claflin Diamonds shares. Those she found she wanted very much.

'I had a duty to tell you within three months of probate,' he agreed. 'Probate was granted three weeks ago.'

'Drag the process out, did you?'

'Yes.'

'I bet you were tempted to destroy the will.'

He smiled grimly. 'It was a non-starter— without a legally valid will, the English laws of intestacy would have taken effect and as his closest living relative, you would have inherited everything anyway, including his share of the business. I had no proof he'd promised me those shares, only my word.'

'Which wasn't worth the paper it was written on,' she supplied.

*'Esattamente.'*

'But if you hadn't learned that destroying the will scuppered all your chances of getting your sticky mitts on the shares, you would have shredded it?'

'I told you, I looked into every eventuality and scenario.'

She smiled serenely. 'He stitched you up like a kipper.'

His forehead furrowed in confusion.

She leaned forwards, her smile widening as a lightness cleared her brain. 'Stitched you up like a kipper. It means he played you. He promised you his shares of the business but then put a condition on it with a set time limit that should have been impossible to fulfil.' Would have been if Enzo hadn't played her so well. 'Non-fulfilment of the condition meant the shares transferred into the hands of someone else—*moi*—and you lost. On top of that, as he'd put you in charge of fulfilling his wishes, your failure to comply meant you would have been in charge of your own failure.'

He acknowledged this truth with a small but sharp nod.

If Rebecca wasn't the pawn in this sick game between two rich men, she would have found her grandfather's underhand methods against Enzo hilarious. It was nothing less than he deserved, something her grandfather must have thought too, else why play such a trick on him? 'He must have had one warped sense of humour to play you like that.'

'I never saw it when he was alive.'

'Were you close to him?'

It was only because she was watching him so studiously for signs of lies that she caught the flicker of emotion on his face. 'Yes.'

'And he did the dirty on you? Ouch.' Yes. *Hilarious*. If her heart wasn't still packed with the weight of her own emotions, she'd be holding her sides with unrestrained glee.

Handsome features taut, he poured himself another drink.

Still smiling, Rebecca took a sip of her gin, briefly averting her eyes so she didn't have to watch the generous mouth that had kissed her with such passion close around the crystal tumbler and the strong, tanned neck she'd adored dragging her lips over throwing itself back to admit the alcohol down it or see his throat moving as the liquid slid down his oesophagus.

When it was safe to look back at him, she said, 'So your failure to marry me means that come midnight, half the business you played such a major part in making a success and is such a vital component of your main business belongs to me, and as probate's been granted and you're the executor, it's your job to hand the shares for it over to me.'

He rubbed his head wearily as he nodded another agreement. It was the executor's duty to deal with all the deceased's assets and either cash them in for the beneficiary—in this case, Rebecca—or transfer them directly into the beneficiary's name.

'*Eccellente*,' she said in her best Italian. Sitting upright, she flashed him her very widest smile. 'Now that I understand the situation even better, I shall wait here until midnight and have the pleasure of you handing those shares directly to mc.'

Though his stare held hers without flickering, for the first time since her interrogation had started, Enzo didn't immediately respond.

'You'd better not be thinking about how you're going to get out of giving them to me,' she said sweetly. 'If I've learned one thing since meeting you it's that the press are like bloodhounds. I imagine they'll stay camped outside until one of us leaves and they get the picture they need, or until one of us—*moi*—goes out and tells them how the ethical philanthropist Enzo Beresi was only marrying the English teacher because he wanted her inheritance.'

That's what had ignited such press interest in Rebecca—her job. Okay, the world's media would have been all over any woman

Enzo had become engaged to, but that one of Europe's richest and most eligible bachelors had fallen for a nobody primary schoolteacher had taken it to a whole other level. No wonder Enzo had thrown his money into protecting her from them, issuing writs left, right and centre ordering them to leave her alone. She'd believed he was protecting her but all along he'd been protecting himself from any journalist discovering the link to her grandfather. Yet another lie.

Long fingers she'd imagined stroking every inch of her body tightened around his crystal tumbler. When his light brown eyes locked on to hers, regret—no doubt because he'd lost—blazed from them. 'I'm sorrier than you can know.'

She waved an airy hand. 'Easy words to say.'

An edge crept into his voice. 'Have I given you any reason to think I'm lying since we started this conversation?'

'Enzo, every word you've said to me in the five months I've known you has been a lie. You're so good at it you'd make Pinocchio feel like an amateur.'

'I have never lied about my feelings for you.'

All the amusement at her grandfather's

dirty trick that had been hurtling through her flattened in an instant. 'Say that one more time and I'll give my share of the business straight to a dog charity.' She would do it too. She could not bear the fake sincerity in his velvet voice. Could not bear how she still ached to believe it. Could not bear how her body was still so acutely aware of him. Could not bear to be reminded of how completely she'd fallen into his web of deceit.

'Midnight,' she added before he could speak. 'I want the shares in my name at midnight.'

His stare didn't waver. 'Impossible.'

'You're Enzo Beresi. Nothing is impossible.' This was the man who'd landed his helicopter on her school's playing field at the end of the school day just so he could whisk her to Monaco for the evening, the man who'd magicked the best seats in the house for the opening of a sell-out Broadway musical she'd mentioned in passing that she quite fancied watching at some point. Before the musical, he'd also conjured up a table in New York's most exclusive restaurant, one that boasted of being fully booked for the next three years. This was the man who, with one call on a Friday evening about the prototype of a new sports car he was interested in, had it delivered from Germany to his Florentine villa by the time he'd woken early the next morning.

'It cannot be done,' he refuted. 'I will need twenty-four hours. Longer. Tomorrow is Sunday.'

'Midnight.'

'I am telling you, Rebecca, I need twenty-four hours.'

The pang in her heart rippled painfully. 'I have already told you not to say my name.'

'Then how do I address you?' he demanded with another flash of anger. In all the months she'd known him, Enzo had always kept tight control of his moods, rarely displaying any sign of temper and never directed at her. The shell of charming perfection he'd always presented to her had well and truly slipped off him and she was glad of it. Glad because it meant he was truly feeling the loss of the game he'd been playing at her expense.

Whatever he was feeling wasn't an ounce of the agony he was putting her through.

'You can address me in the same way my pupils do—as Miss Foley.' She looked at her watch. Nearly eight p.m. She could hardly believe how quickly time was passing. 'Eight a.m. That's my final offer.'

'It can't be done by eight a.m. Give me until three.'

'Twelve.'

'One o'clock. I will have the shares transferred into your name by one o'clock tomorrow afternoon.'

She folded her arms tightly around her chest, hating that she was thrown back to the day they'd negotiated the date of their wedding and all the reasons she'd believed he wanted to marry her so quickly.

But she had never *truly* believed them, had she? That nagging voice of doubt had always warned her she was just too plain and ordinary for a man as worldly and glamorous as Enzo Beresi.

'Okay. One o'clock. But I wait here until it's done.' Not only because she didn't trust him but to make him suffer her company with the full knowledge that he'd lost and that she was going to go skipping into the sunset with the very thing he'd fought so hard and so dirty to keep from her hands.

The flicker on his features before he nodded was unmistakable.

'And if you're one minute late getting it done then...' She snapped her fingers and smiled. 'I go outside to the press and sing like a canary.'

An hour after Rebecca had spontaneously decided to torment Enzo by camping in his villa until the shares of her grandfather's business were legally hers, and serious regret had kicked in.

Immersed in her tiny little mini power trip, she'd forgotten the reasons why she'd been so desperate to flee.

As soon as they'd agreed on a time for Enzo to get the shares transferred into her name he'd disappeared to get things in motion. She'd been left staring at the walls of the room he'd proposed to her in ever since.

Before she'd moved in a week ago, when the school year had come to an end, Rebecca had visited this villa a grand total of six times. She couldn't remember her first real impression of the villa Enzo called home. She'd been too stunned at being flown to Florence in a private jet and then amazed at the scale and richness of his home for any real thoughts to penetrate. She'd known he was rich but hadn't comprehended *how* rich. The next evening, he'd proposed…

She yanked at her hair so hard that when she moved her hand away, blond strands had woven between her fingers. She would *not* think of his proposal, or how he'd had to ask her three times before she'd grasped what he was saying.

'Why?' she'd asked dumbly.

Why, why, why, why, why. The story of her entire relationship with him.

'Because I can't imagine my life without you in it,' he'd replied with a sincerity she'd believed.

Once they were engaged, she'd given up trying to comprehend and instead let her imagination run riot. In her mind, children had popped out of her in a procession of love, this richly imposing villa with its abundance of glass and marble slowly transforming into a nursery filled with tattle-tales and hair pulling and scratching and biting and cuddles and giggles and mischief. They'd spent much time together in his London penthouse and Enzo had taken her for long weekends to his apartment overlooking Times Square in New

York, but it was here in Florence that they would live and raise their family.

Unable to bear the memories and broken dreams any longer, she headed outside into the balmy evening.

*I can't imagine my life without you*, she mimicked under her breath as she stomped past the secluded swimming pool and the clay tennis court to the vast landscaped grounds at the rear of the villa. The cicadas had just stopped singing for the day, so the only sound was the gentle breeze rustling through the trees that formed the perimeter of Enzo's grounds and ensured absolute privacy.

At the far end, hidden from the villa, was a hanging double egg seat. Rebecca barely glanced at it as she parked her bottom on the curved marble bench close by. Three nights ago she'd sat on that egg seat with Enzo, her legs hooked over his thighs, trying her best to tempt him into making love to her as the seat gently swung them. It made her core throb to remember how she'd cupped his straining hardness through his trousers, rubbed her nose along his throat inhaling his delicious woody cologne, and provocatively whispered—

'There you are.'

Shoulders sagging, she closed her eyes and swallowed the lump in her throat. It took every ounce of resilience to evoke nonchalance into her voice. 'Here I am. Have you started the process?'

'Yes.' He sat at the other end of the bench, far enough away that there was no danger of their bodies accidentally touching. But not far enough to stop his alluring scent from dancing into her airways.

Awareness threading through every part of her, she crossed her legs tightly. 'Nothing else you need to do for it?'

'For now, everything is in hand.'

It had to be the night air magnifying the effect of him, heightening her awareness, making her yearn to close the distance between them and...

Unable to bear it, she jumped to her feet and made to leave. 'Good.'

Before she could escape him, he said, 'I have had the possessions you left at the hotel delivered here.'

Images of the sheer white negligée she'd planned to wear that night flittered into her mind's eye. She quickly blinked it away and said stiffly, 'Thank you.'

'They have also sent me CCTV footage of the woman who delivered the package to you.'

'I've told you already, I don't care.'

'It was my mother.'

# CHAPTER FOUR

REBECCA'S HEART THUMPED at this. Her mind jumped to the svelte raven-haired woman who'd welcomed her into her palatial home with a warm embrace that had touched her heart and eased her fears. She doubted anyone met their future in-laws without a smidgeon of panic and Silvana Beresi had gone out of her way to make Rebecca feel welcome…

Her thumping heart changed direction and plummeted as the implications of what Enzo had just told her suddenly made themselves clear.

She turned to face him. 'Your mother?'

His back was ramrod straight, palms pressed down firmly by his thighs, splayed fingers gripping the bench. He gave a brief, grim nod.

'Your *mother*?'

Another, terser nod.

'But...' She swallowed and shook her head. 'She helped choose the design for my wedding dress. She helped plan the menu. She chose the wines to pair with each course.' Rebecca was aware of an hysterical tinge coming into her voice but could do nothing to stop it. 'She lent me her grandmother's wedding tiara for my something borrowed! Why would she do all that and then sabotage everything at the last minute? It makes no sense. Why would she do all that if she didn't want me to marry you?'

'You misunderstand her motives,' he said emotionlessly. 'She had no objection to you marrying me. She objected to me marrying *you* under what she considered to be a falsehood.'

'*Why*? She must have known what would happen.' She slammed her hand to her chest in a futile attempt to control a heart that had lost the ability to thump rhythmically. If it had been anyone else but his mother she'd be cheering them to the rafters and planning the delivery of a crate of champagne as a thank you. But his mother? His own *mother*?

His nod that time was so sharp it could slice butter.

'She knew I wouldn't go through with the wedding?'

'She never does anything without considering every eventuality. In that respect, I am my mother's son.'

'But...' But Rebecca's overloaded mind had gone blank. Legs feeling like noodles, she dropped onto the egg chair and tried to make sense of her thoughts.

Enzo's deep, velvet voice laced with bitterness broke the silence. 'Telling her was a mistake on my part.'

'Then why did you?' she whispered.

His gaze searched hers through the violet sky. 'Guilt.'

Her laughter was unbidden and tart. 'Guilt? You? Now I've heard everything.'

He was on his feet and standing in front of her before she could even blink.

The emerging moonlight made the bronze of his skin more marble-like than ever, his beautiful bone structure carved slashes by the sculptor who'd created him... But the hand that clasped hers was warm flesh and the blaze in his eyes a reminder of the passion that lurked beneath that sculpted surface.

Leaning his face into hers, his taut features

became darkly animated. 'Look into my eyes and tell me I am lying.'

The heat from Enzo's breath matched the look in his eyes, and for an impossibly long moment Rebecca found herself caught in the magnetism that had ensnared her all those months ago from the very first glance. Ensnared her completely. Her pulses jumping, the ache deep in her pelvis that had started when he'd entered her life flared with brilliant, needy colour but as her gaze drifted down to his mouth, a sharpness tightened in her chest and she snatched her hand away.

Turning her face away too, she said with as much strength as she could muster, 'I thought we'd already established that your Pinocchio skills are top-notch.'

A finger brushed her cheek bone. An involuntary shiver laced her spine, and she had to clench her hands into fists to stop them reaching to wrap around him, and tighten her core to stop herself leaning forwards to press her cheek against the comfort of his solid chest. So many evenings spent wrapped in his arms, her body fizzing with unfulfilled desire but the strong, rhythmic thuds of his heart against her ear making the heat of it bearable. In his arms, Rebecca had felt a sense of safety that had been missing since her parents' deaths. Enzo had unshackled the chains of her grief and given her the tools to see beyond the day to tomorrow. He'd given her an anchor to the world she hadn't known she'd become unmoored from.

And now she was rudderless again. The anchor had been nothing but an illusion.

He stepped away from her. From the corner of her eye she saw him sit on the lawn facing her.

When she finally dared to look at him, the expression on his face turned the tightness in her chest into a physical pain.

Long legs stretched out before him, he'd propped himself semi-upright with his hands flat on the ground behind him, his black T-shirt straining over his muscular torso. Gazing at her, he quietly said, 'If I could do it all again I would do it differently. There would be no lies.'

Her chest hurt too much for the retort she wanted to throw at him to form.

His lips twitched then twisted into a grim smile. 'I told my mother the truth the night before you moved here.'

'You mean the night before I quit my career and the only home I've known so I could move to a country whose language I don't speak.'

He inclined his head slowly. '*Sì*. I knew what you were giving up. The closer the day got, the more I felt it.'

'Felt what?' She wanted him to spell out exactly how his guilt had felt to him. Maybe he could spell it sufficiently well that she actually believed it.

'The…' He grasped for the right word. 'Magnitude?'

Enzo's T-shirt had risen up, exposing his naked navel. Thick dark hair arrowed down to the belt of his jeans. A rush of heated awareness flooding her, Rebecca hastily averted her eyes.

That was all she'd ever seen of his naked form before. Odd snatches. That was all he'd ever allowed.

'I'm the last person to ask how you felt.'

'I never…' He cut himself off and took a deep breath before saying, 'It had become this huge weight inside me. My guilt. It was too late to tell you the truth. I couldn't risk losing you.'

'Couldn't risk losing the shares, you mean,' she muttered, bringing her knees to her chest and closing her arms around them, and wishing with all her might that she wasn't aching for Enzo's arms to be around her.

His gaze didn't falter. 'No. I stopped caring about the shares when I fell in l—'

'Don't you dare,' she interrupted shakily, blinking back another surge of hot tears. 'Just don't. I've already told you. Any more talk about love or feelings and I will destroy the business by any means I can find.'

He contemplated her with an expression she couldn't dissect. 'I've hurt you very badly.'

She brushed away the one tear that had broken free. 'You've ripped my heart out.'

He winced, jaw clenching.

Afraid he'd use this as an excuse for more worthless apologies, she swallowed before adding, 'I don't want to talk about my feelings any more than I want to hear more lies about yours. You've played me like a cat with a mouse for the sake of the shares and I will not let you play me again. If you have even an ounce of feelings for me then give me your word—no more talk of them or I swear I will do my best to destroy *everything*.'

His stare penetrated her through the encroaching darkness. Eventually, he sighed. 'You have my word.'

Throat suddenly choked, Rebecca nodded her acknowledgement.

'But not because of your threats,' he added, his gaze still fixed intently on her. 'Even if I believed you would go ahead with it—and I do not underestimate that your pain and anger could lead you to do it—I give you my word because there is nothing I would not do to put right what I've done to you.'

The silence that followed this was profound, filled with an agonising tension that added weight to the pain in Rebecca's chest. Knowing the emotions she sensed emanating from Enzo were nothing but a figment of her imagination only made it harder to endure. They had as much value as his words.

Such fine words. Such cheap words. Words that cost nothing to say but everything to hear.

'So you confided the truth in your mother,' she prompted quietly, bringing the conversation back on track.

Enzo stretched his neck back before lifting his head again to look at her. He grimaced. 'A mistake.'

'Not from my perspective.'

He pulled a face. 'I should have remembered her contradictory morality. Alcohol loosens lips and that night I'd drunk more than I should.'

Unsure what he meant, Rebecca's eyebrows pinched together.

His eyes continued to penetrate. 'I have not been completely open with you about my mother or my relationship with her.'

'You do surprise me.'

A tiny flash of amusement twitched at the corners of his lips at her sarcasm. 'When I first pursued you, I wanted nothing to make you think I was less than perfect. Getting those shares was too important to me. I could not risk you having any doubts about me or the family you were marrying into.'

So his seeming perfection *had* been an act. Of course, she already knew this, but to hear it from his own mouth managed to make her feel both wretched and relieved. In many ways, Enzo's perfection had awed her more than his wealth and lifestyle but to think everything he'd done for her, all the little things from filling a hot water bottle to help soothe her period cramps to giving her a head massage to soothe away the stress after a particularly difficult meeting with a parent whose child had been caught repeatedly hitting another child who refused to play with him, had all been so calculated… Oh, but that made her heart shrivel.

Clearing her throat that had closed up again, she flippantly said, 'Is your mother some kind of criminal or something?'

'Was. But not in the convicted sense. Let me put it this way—the jewellery she traded did not always have the cleanest of provenances.'

His answer was so unexpected that Rebecca felt the strangest compulsion to laugh.

As his mother had retired into being a lady of leisure before Enzo had tricked his way into her life, Rebecca knew little about Silvana's business other than that she'd been a hugely successful international trader of jewels and that growing up in that world had inspired Silvana's only child to make his own forays into the jewellery business. He'd freely admitted to her that his mother's advice on the trade and the nuggets he'd picked up over the years had been invaluable to him when opening his first store. Any mistakes made had been his own.

What he'd failed to mention was that buying into her grandfather's diamond business had been the biggest component in his success, a thought that quickly killed the bubbling laughter.

'Are we talking stolen jewels?' She watched his reaction carefully.

He raised a shoulder. 'Nothing identifiably stolen. To any external observer, she ran a clean business. She only traded items with origins that had the correct supporting paperwork or could not be identified—nothing that would get flagged up on a database of stolen items for example.'

'But you think she did trade them?'

'I know she traded them, just as I know she had certain jewels stolen to order.'

'How does that work? Surely they'd go on that database you just mentioned?'

'If you know what you are doing, it is not difficult to remove gems from their settings and melt gold.'

'You have proof she did this?'

'None. But I'm her son. I travelled the world with her. I learned the signs. I am not a believer of coincidence.'

She wanted to scratch her head. 'Right, so your mother's a retired criminal mastermind.'

'Yes.'

'That explains you then.'

His handsome features tightened. It should please her, his obvious dislike that she should make that comparison between mother and son.

'I understand why you might think that but I grew up in constant fear of my mother's criminality being discovered and her being dragged away by the police or Interpol. There was never a chance I would follow in her footsteps. I can account for the provenance of every item ever sold in all of my stores. I run a clean business. I employ a team who do due diligence on every business I look to invest in and on-the-spot checks to ensure the businesses are being run legally and ethically.'

'Then what changed? If you've never broken the law before or allowed unethical behaviour in your businesses, why try to steal my inheritance?'

'I didn't try to steal it, damn it.' He punched the lawn in frustration. 'I always intended for you to have the cash value of the shares.'

'Which is?'

'Claflin Diamonds is currently valued at one hundred million.'

Five months ago it was a figure that would likely have made her faint. 'What's the rest of my grandfather's estate worth?'

'Including property, twenty million.'

'So come midnight I'm going to be worth seventy million euros?'

'Pounds.'

She let that sink in. Seventy million pounds.

'Woo-hoo,' she said flatly. 'I'm going to be rich…' There was not a cat in hell's chance she would keep the money. It made her feel dirty just to imagine it. 'Although still a pauper compared to you.' Adding a few zeros to the end of the sum gave a ballpark figure of what Enzo was worth. 'Supposing I take at face value that you intended to give me the cash value of my half of the business, that still doesn't explain how you could go against the strong ethics you expect me and the world to believe you possess and do what you did to me.'

'At the time, I told myself it was the principle.'

'*You* have principles? Very funny.'

He closed his eyes and took a long breath. 'Reb… Miss Foley,' he corrected, speaking slowly. Wearily.

'What?' she asked when he didn't say anything further.

He shook his head and sighed. 'I was going to ask you to stop the sniping at me but I cannot blame you for being like this. It is nothing I don't deserve.'

'Oh, stop playing the martyr,' she muttered, squirming, unable to understand why she should feel guilty for her sniping when, if Enzo's mother hadn't ratted him out, they would at this very minute be newlyweds looking to escape their wedding reception so they could make love for the first time.

She wanted to open her mouth and scream. Right at this moment she should be delirious with happiness celebrating her marriage to the love of her life and the man of her dreams.

Dreams that had been made entirely of smoke.

She swallowed back the heavy wave of nausea rising up her throat and strove for strength in her voice. 'Going back to your mother... You were telling me about her criminal masterminding ways and contradictory morality.' Strangely enough, it took no stretch of the imagination to imagine Silvana as a criminal mastermind, not in the way it did to imagine Enzo as being like that.

'Let me give you an example. You have heard of the Hollywood producer Rico Roberts? He was accused of groping young actresses last year. There were voice recordings.'

'It rings a vague bell.'

'Six years ago, two million dollars' worth of jewellery was stolen from Rico's LA home while he and his wife were at a movie premiere.'

'Your mother?'

'She was in Florence at the time but they were stolen on her orders, I am certain of it. She had met Rico and his wife at a party some years before the break-in and took a dislike to them. Rumours that he was a sex pest had circulated for years but until the recent scandal, there was no proof and he was too big a player in the movie industry to bring down without concrete evidence. Those were the kinds of rich people my mother targeted. People she didn't have to feel guilt over.'

'A modern-day Robina Hood?'

The corners of his lips twitched again. 'Yes, but with the proceeds only filling her own coffers. If she had liked Rico and disbelieved the rumours then I am certain he and his wife would still be in full possession of their jewellery collection. I am certain that if she'd been presented with an opportunity to steal from someone she knew and liked, and given a cast-iron guarantee that she would get away with it, she would have refused. If she decides she likes someone then she will be their friend for life. And you, Miss Foley, she likes.'

'I'm flattered,' she said drolly and was rewarded with a widening of Enzo's mouth and a flash of his dimples.

'You should be. She's never liked any of my other lovers.'

The lightening of the atmosphere came crashing down. 'We were never lovers,' Rebecca said, trying hard to keep the hurt from her voice. 'I suppose that's one thing I should thank you for, that you never let it go that far. I don't think I could cope knowing you'd made love to me on a lie too.'

Her cheeks scalded to think of all the times she'd begged him to make love to her, her hunger for him the flame of a lit candle whose wick never tapered even when they were apart.

What, she wondered desperately, would it take to douse the flame? Because even now, with Enzo's lies exposed, the flame burned as brightly as it ever had, the sticky heat of arousal and awareness as thick in her as it had ever been.

Enzo had induced the flame. Deliberately. He'd fed it and nurtured it and stoked it.

She couldn't hate him more.

'Why do you think I never allowed it to happen between us?'

'Because you didn't have to.' Bitterness crept back into her tone. 'I guess you didn't want me enough. As soon as you established I was a virgin you used it as an excuse not to—'

He sprang from a recline to his haunches before she could finish her sentence.

'Yes,' he said savagely, hands pressed down on the padded egg chair either side of her hips, eyes boring deep into hers. 'I used it as an excuse because I had to. When I first set out to seduce you into marrying me, I told myself you were your grandfather's blood and likely to be as devious as him. You can have no idea the depth of betrayal I felt when I read his will. I didn't think of you as a person but as an obstacle, and an underserving obstacle at that—you'd never met him and had turned down his requests to meet. You returned his cards and cheques. You'd made it clear you wanted nothing to do with him or his money and still he left you everything, including the half of our shared business that he'd promised me; that he *owed* me. Believe me, I was prepared to hate you in the flesh as much as I hated the very idea of you and when I met you it was a relief to find you attractive enough to not have to fake desire for you along with everything else.'

Somehow, while he'd been making his biting but impassioned speech, Enzo's hands had taken hold of Rebecca's waist. Trying desperately not to fall into the hypnotic swirl of his eyes was as impossible as telling her flesh not to react to his grip on her, the ache at his touch too strong for her to find the sense needed to shove his hands off and push him away as she knew she should. She'd been a slave to his touch from their very first kiss.

His fingers tightened their grip, the tip of his nose almost touching hers. 'Do you remember our first date? By the end of it…' He sucked a sharp breath in through his teeth. '*Dio*, you can have no idea how sexy you are. The way your lips move when you eat…' His eyes flashed. 'But as soon as you told me you were a virgin it changed everything for me. It didn't matter how much I wanted you—I knew on a fundamental level that making love to you on a lie was unforgivable.'

Fighting with everything she had against the tumult of emotions Enzo's words and closeness had induced, Rebecca had to plead with herself not to fall into the trap he was laying, to keep her hands tightly fisted at her sides, to stop herself inhaling too deeply so his divine scent couldn't snake its way down to her lungs and tip her over the edge.

'What about our wedding night?' she whispered raggedly. 'Would you have gone ahead with it without telling me the truth?'

'Yes.'

'Even though it would have still been unforgivable, what with it still being based on the same lie?'

'Yes. Because by then you would have been my wife and tied to me, and I would never have let you go.'

And then his mouth found hers.

# CHAPTER FIVE

REBECCA'S FISTS WERE clenched so tightly in her vain attempt to keep her lips clamped and airways closed that her nails dug sharply into her palms.

There was nothing she could do to stop the violent trembling of her body or the thumping tattoo of her heart against her ribs. Those reactions were involuntary and completely beyond her control; physical reactions fighting with equal ferocity to the sane part of her brain pleading with her mouth to stay clamped and not give in to the desperate, burning ache for him.

*Don't give in*, she begged herself. *This means nothing to him. It was all a set-up from the very start.*

Her pleading words to herself penetrated the memory of the very start and threw her back to the night she'd come out into this garden to forget. The night Enzo proposed.

He'd taken her out to dinner on the river, an exclusive floating restaurant where they were served the most exquisite food she'd ever tasted. After a dessert of chocolate mousse on a chocolate crumb with flakes of gold leaf scattered over it, they'd taken their after-dinner liqueurs onto the top deck. The cloudless evening sky had been chilly. Noticing her shiver, Enzo had draped his suit jacket over her shoulders...how she had *thrilled* at the pleasure of being warmed by the remnants of his body heat. By the time they'd returned to the villa, Rebecca had been floating like the boat they'd dined on in a sea of happiness she'd never known before.

She'd smelt the roses from the moment she stepped through the front door.

Hundreds and hundreds of red roses encircled the main living room, set in so many crystal vases Florence must have declared a shortage. There, in the centre of the room, a plinth had been placed. On it, the largest vase of all. Wrapped around it had been a red ribbon onto which had been tied a small black velvet box.

Enzo had been the one to untie it. He'd

held it in his hand and sank onto one knee before her.

Her heart had beat so hard and so fast she'd feared she would be sick.

He'd opened the lid. Inside it glittered the most beautiful oval diamond ring.

'Will you marry me?'

Three times he'd asked the question before what he was asking actually sank in, and even then she couldn't comprehend it or comprehend what was happening to her. Barely a month before, Rebecca's world had been grey with grief but then Enzo had come into her life and saturated it with colour and now he was asking her to marry him?

'Why?' It was the only word she could form in her brain or on her tongue. Why her when he could have anyone?

His eyes had glittered. 'Because I can't imagine my life without you in it.'

And still she'd gawped at him, hardly daring to believe this could be true and that she wasn't dreaming.

He'd risen to his feet slowly and taken her hand, and suddenly she'd detected something new in his eyes, something she could never in a hundred years explain but when he'd then quietly said, 'What do you say? Will you marry me, Rebecca?' her heart had exploded with joy.

'Yes.'

Such a contortion of emotions had flashed over his face that she'd been certain she'd only imagined the shadow that darkened it before the heartbreaking smile she'd fallen in love with widened his whole face and he pulled her into his arms for a kiss so deep and passionate that the pulses in her core throbbed throughout her entire body.

He'd broken the kiss to cup her face in his hands. 'I love you, Rebecca.' There had been a dazed quality to his voice that matched the dizziness she'd been feeling. 'I love you.'

To know it had all been fake, every last part of it, broke her heart all over again and gave her the impetus needed to turn her cheek and wrench her mouth from his with a plaintive, '*Stop!*'

The wonderful pressure of Enzo's mouth against hers disappeared leaving nothing but tingles on her lips. The grip on her waist loosened and then disappeared too but the heat from his body remained as he covered her fists, a gentle, tender pressure that made her want to cry harder than anything else had that whole day.

'My desire for you was never a lie,' he said fervently.

She shook her head violently. 'Stop *lying* to me. I told you, I don't want to hear this.'

'Why would I lie about this? What purpose would it serve?' He pressed her hand to his chest. 'I've already lost you. But you haven't lost me. Everything I—' He cut himself off and swore under his breath. Gritting his teeth, he squeezed her fisted hand tighter against his heart and said, 'Whatever you believe of me, never think I didn't want you. Resisting you is the hardest thing I have done in my life.'

How could she wish so hard to believe him when *everything* was predicated on a lie?

Another memory slammed into her, straddling Enzo on the loveseat of his New York penthouse, both fully clothed, their pelvises locked together, the rock solidness of his erection burning, tantalising and frustrating her in equal measure. She'd been desperate for him to make love to her. 'I've spent my whole life waiting to feel like this,' she'd whispered into his ear.

His kiss had been deep and hard, and then he'd fisted her hair in his hands and tugged her head back to gaze deep into her eyes.

'What I feel for you is like nothing I have felt before.'

'Then make love to me,' she'd pleaded.

He'd kissed her again, fervently. '*Cara*, there is nothing I want more than to carry you to my bed and make love to you but our wedding is so close now. Let every part of our day be special. We have the rest of our lives to satisfy our desires.'

She closed her eyes to the memories and shook her head even harder. 'Please, Enzo, just accept that you've lost. You're demeaning us both.'

'Do you really think so little of yourself?' he demanded.

'It's nothing to do with how I see myself but how I see you, and how I see you is as a ruthless liar prepared to do anything and say anything to get what he wants.'

Hands suddenly abandoned her fists and cupped her cheeks. Rebecca squeezed her closed eyes even tighter.

'If it is nothing to do with how you see yourself then why are you so willing to accept that everything including my desire was a lie?' he asked savagely, his breath hot on her face. '*Dio*, I do not believe there's a man alive who—' The abruptness with which he cut himself off this time was matched only by the swift release of her cheeks and the removal of his heat.

She opened her eyes as he rose to his feet. Dragging his fingers through his hair, he shook his head before landing his gaze back on her. 'You never believed in me, did you?'

With the chill that had replaced the warmth of his body having stolen her breath, Rebecca could only gape at him.

His firm yet generous lips twitched before a short bark of laugher escaped them. 'Or is it better to say you never believed in yourself? I remember when I proposed, you kept asking, 'Why? Why me?' I didn't know you like I do now and I thought you were putting on an act, but you were being genuine, weren't you? You have such low esteem that your first thought when receiving a marriage proposal was to ask why—'

'Turns out I was right to ask that,' she interrupted shakily.

His brow drew into a disbelieving line. 'Would you have asked the question if you had confidence in yourself? You are beautiful and smart and funny but I think of all the times we went out and you were always worried you didn't look good enough or would show me up, and I think too of how frightened you were to meet my mother because you were afraid she would think you weren't good enough...'

Rebecca's heart was thrashing wildly against her ribs. 'Stop twisting things. This isn't about me, this is about you.'

Another bark of laughter and a widening of his mouth into a smile that contained more bitterness than warmth. 'Without you there is no me, don't you understand that? If your insecurities hadn't made you question yourself so much, you would already know it and not only understand but feel right *here*,' he punched a fist into his chest, 'that as big a bastard as I am and as terrible as my behaviour has been, not everything was a lie.'

How she wished it was possible to close her ears as easily as it was to close her eyes. She wished even harder that she could close off her emotions and the longing to believe him, but the hard shell she'd managed to erect around herself earlier had softened into mush.

What ordinary woman in her position wouldn't have questioned why a wildly attractive billionaire who could have anyone he wanted would want to marry her? And what ordinary woman wouldn't worry about making a fool of the man she loved when out in the high society world he inhabited and which was so alien to her own that it could have been set on a different planet? She'd thought the hotel they'd met in had been posh? Within days of that meeting, Rebecca's definition of posh had been blown out of the water. Compared to the places Enzo had taken her to, that hotel had been a rundown dive. She, a primary schoolteacher who, apart from her university years, had lived her whole life in the same end-of-terrace house in the suburbs was suddenly thrown into a world of glamour and limousines, Michelin-starred restaurants and private member clubs. If she'd actually engaged her brain and thought back to that first meeting, she'd have realised that something about it was all wrong, that there was no way Enzo, whose London offices were in the capital's highest skyscraper, would conduct business in such an ordinary place.

But she'd been too caught up in the glamour and the awakening of feelings smothered for so long she'd forgotten they even existed in her. Feelings like happiness.

Being with Enzo had made her so happy. The grimace that had been so much of a feature since they'd been holed up in the villa returned to his face at her silence. 'I'm going to get something to eat.'

She stared at him blankly at the sudden change of subject.

He took a visible, deep breath. 'It is getting very late. I have not eaten all day. I don't imagine you have either. Do not starve yourself out of spite of me.'

Turning, he set off towards the villa, but had only taken five paces before he stopped and twisted back to face her. 'One other thing. If I really was prepared to do anything to get those shares, as you seem to think, I would have made love to you every single time you begged it of me.'

When Enzo's tall frame had disappeared into the shadows, Rebecca flopped back into the curved support of the egg seat, then drew her knees to her chest and wrapped her arms around herself. Her cheeks were still enflamed from his parting shot, her stomach so tight and cramped she didn't think she would ever desire food again.

If only her desire and feelings for him could be so easily switched off.

She'd been an idiot for thinking she could

maintain her hard shell and survive the night here without hurting herself further. Having Enzo personally hand over the shares he'd coveted so badly wasn't worth what being with him did to her.

She'd lost count of the times she'd begged him to make love to her, and for him to throw that back at her was mortifying and cruel.

But there had been no cruelty in his matter-of-fact delivery.

If he was telling the truth then his refusal to make love to her had been as agonising for him as it had been for her.

The worst of it was that she did believe he was telling the truth on this. It had been the fevered sincerity that had blazed from his eyes; and she hugged herself harder, knowing she mustn't think like this. If she accepted this one part of their relationship as the truth then what else would her foolish heart beg her to accept? That he did love her? And what excuses would her foolish heart start making for him then? Would it make her think he'd been perfectly justified in lying about absolutely everything? Would it make her think he had a point about her never believing in herself? Would her foolish heart make her gaslight herself?

She rubbed her chin into her knee. She really should have followed her initial instincts and headed straight to the airport. She might be home by now and not sat in Enzo's garden...

Home? She almost laughed. She didn't have a home any more. Not one she could live in. She'd signed a tenancy agreement before she'd moved to Italy. A newlywed couple were now living in the only home she'd ever known and were legally entitled to stay there for a year.

A place to live was just one of the many things she would have to sort out when she returned to England. Finding herself a job was another. Her replacement had already been appointed, and her heart swelled painfully to realise all her now ex-colleagues had witnessed her jilt Enzo at the altar. He'd paid for them to fly over and paid for their accommodation. He'd paid the expenses of every friend and family member she'd included on the guest list.

Rebecca sprang off the egg seat and blinked furiously against yet another batch of hot tears. She didn't want to remember Enzo's incredible generosity, all brought about when she'd voiced doubts about marrying in Florence because the price might prohibit many of those she wanted to be there from attending. He was generous to a fault, and she didn't think it was an act. He had more money than he could ever hope to spend in a thousand lifetimes and donated a set percentage of his annual income to various children's and animal charities, a philanthropy that predated her entry into his life by many years.

Acknowledging this only made his treatment of her harder to understand. How could a man with such a generous heart be capable of such deviousness, and as she followed his footsteps and slipped back into the villa, her chest tightened and she found herself wishing almost as hard as she'd wished that the oncologist's diagnosis of her mother's cancer was wrong that Enzo had convincingly denied that everything between them had been staged. Wished he'd successfully given her a plausible explanation for everything.

But there had been no denial or plausible explanation. He'd pleaded guilty and she would not gaslight herself into believing anything else.

All her stuff from the hotel had been left by the front door with the rest of her belongings. Silence surrounded her. Wherever Enzo was in the villa, he wasn't close by.

Her phone was in the handbag she'd left at the hotel and she pulled it out, in two minds over whether to call for a taxi and leave immediately.

No, she decided. She didn't see how she could return to England and rebuild her life if she still had unanswered questions. There were some things it was impossible to move on from and if she hadn't lived through the death of both her parents within days of each other, she doubted she'd ever be able to recover from this.

One thing Rebecca had learned in those dark, bottomless days had been that unanswered questions could drive you crazy. Her father's death had been straightforward in the respect that he'd suffered a massive heart attack. There had been no ambiguity to it. Her mother's death, though, might have been prevented if their local doctor had taken her symptoms more seriously instead of fobbing her off with things like calcium deficiency and menopause. It was the *might* in the equation that had turned Rebecca into a red-eyed insomniac, because that was the part no one could definitively answer. If their doctor had arranged a full range of blood tests when she'd first gone to see him two years before her death about being constantly tired, if her mum hadn't accepted that her symptoms were consistent with the menopause and ignored that she was bruising easily... All the *ifs* that led to the *mights*, because there was no way of knowing if her mum would still be alive even if she'd been diagnosed sooner. She *might* have lived another five years. She *might* have made it to old bones.

It had taken a full year for Rebecca to accept the diagnosis question could never be answered. She wasn't prepared to tear herself apart with unanswered questions again. Not when her only means of answering them would be through the man she would never set eyes on again after she left this villa.

Rebecca found Enzo in the smaller dining room, the one that only comfortably sat twenty people rather than the one in which he could host a hundred.

He was sat at the far end of the marble table, features set tightly, almost slouched in his chair stabbing a fork into his plate, the light of the chandelier landing like drops of gold on his skin. The scents wafting from his plate sent a hunger pang rippling through her, and a different, stronger pang. It was the scent of his favourite food, a simple layered aubergine, tomato and mozzarella dish, the Enzo Beresi version of comfort food that was the polar opposite of the fancy food he usually ate when dining out.

Of course he was comfort eating. He'd lost; a blow that must be particularly hard to bear for a man who always won at everything.

As soon as he spotted her, his demeanour changed. He straightened. His chest rose, neck extending as he nodded his acknowledgement of her presence.

Leaning into the door's frame, it took effort for Rebecca to make her mouth and throat move. 'I'm going to get something to eat. Wait in here for me?'

His lips a thin line, he inclined his head.

It took more effort to control the next pang that ripped through her when she discovered the chef had prepared her own favourite comfort food of macaroni cheese for her. She didn't need to ask to know he'd made it for her on Enzo's instructions.

Removing it from under the grill, he served it bubbling and golden into a warmed pasta bowl for her and would no doubt have carried it to the dining room if she'd let him. Thanking him, she carried it on a tray back to the dining room and took a seat halfway down the long table. If she sat facing Enzo at the other end to him then she'd have to shout. This way she was close enough to converse but not close enough she risked having any part of her body make contact—accidental or otherwise—with his. Also, being side-on meant she didn't have to look at him unless she wanted to.

It hurt immeasurably that she did want to look. Staring at his gorgeous face was something she'd thought she would never tire of doing.

'Thank you for getting Sal to make this for me,' she said quietly.

'You're welcome.'

She hated the softness in his tone. Hated it and loved it in equal measure, and as she dug her spoon into the gooey mixture, it came to her that she hated and loved *him* in equal measure too.

# CHAPTER SIX

REBECCA'S MUM HAD always described love
and hate as being two sides of the same coin.
She'd known her mum was referring to Rebecca's grandfather when she said this, but
having never hated anyone herself, it was a
concept Rebecca had never fully understood.

She understood it now, sitting in this suddenly claustrophobic dining room. Such were
the emotions crashing through her that if
she'd been standing, the dizziness from it
would have caused her to stumble. Her heart
throbbed painfully, the beats sending needles
of pain through her veins, infecting every
cell in her body.

'Would you like a glass of wine?' he asked
after she'd been sat there for a good minute
without uttering a word.

She nodded without looking at him.

He rose from his seat. 'White?'

She gave another nod. If her grip on the spoon got any tighter the metal would bend.

A few moments later, he placed her glass on the table beside her.

She tensed and held her breath. She'd become conditioned to Enzo never being within a foot of her without touching her in some way, whether a brush of his hand against her back or the drop of a kiss into her hair, and she didn't know if her body was giving signs of relief or distress when he retook his seat without a whisper of physical contact.

When she dared reopen her airways, she breathed in the remnants of his woody cologne, and took a large gulp of her wine in an attempt to drown it. The attempt was a dismal failure. All the questions consuming her were drowned in the sharp but sweet crisp liquid too, her mind a blank and it took more co-ordination than she'd needed since she was a toddler to spoon a mouthful of the meal that usually brought her the greatest comfort between her lips. Whatever Enzo's chef did to make the simple infusion of pasta, milk and cheese into a culinary masterpiece was something she'd been happy to never understand; delirious devotion of its comforting amazingness had been enough.

This time, there was no comfort to be had. She couldn't even taste it.

It didn't help that Enzo's gaze was locked on her. Its burn seeped deep inside her.

'You didn't finish telling me why your mother basically ratted you out to me,' she said when she feared spontaneous combustion from the heat his stare was inducing had become more than a distinct possibility.

From the corner of her eye she saw him take a drink of his red wine, heard him follow the silent swallow with a deep breath. 'No,' he agreed. 'I didn't.'

'I need you to explain what you meant by saying she didn't want you to marry me and not the other way around.'

'My mother does not like many people in this world but, as I said, she likes you. If she could have chosen a daughter-in-law, it would have been you.'

She didn't know how to respond to that. Should she be flattered that a jewellery thief considered her the ideal daughter-in-law?

'She took to you for many of the same reasons I did,' he explained quietly. 'You are genuine. A good person. You wear your heart on your sleeve and speak your mind, which is very refreshing when you are used to being surrounded by calculators.'

Rebecca dipped her spoon back into her bowl. 'Calculators?'

'That is what we call those who want us only for what they can get and calculate every word they say in our company. An in joke I think you call it.'

She swirled the spoon slowly through the thickening sauce. 'That must make you a calculator too, seeing as you calculated every word you ever said to me.'

'I suppose it must,' he agreed. 'But not the words you think. Not once I learned there was no calculation at all in your nature and I—'

He broke himself away from saying what Rebecca instinctively knew would have been more forbidden words about feelings.

'Why would she sabotage our wedding though? It doesn't matter if she liked me or not—you're her son.'

'It was revenge for forcing her to dissolve her business.'

She whipped her head towards him before she could stop herself.

His gaze was already locked on her. Fingers tightly gripped the stem of his wine glass. His handsome features were like granite and when he opened his mouth, his voice had the same stony quality. 'Five years ago I threatened to report her to the authorities. I had enough circumstantial evidence of the robberies she'd masterminded to make them investigate her.'

She blinked her shock at this unexpected twist.

Incredibly, his features hardened even further. 'Someone needed to stop her and that someone was me.'

It took a moment to unfreeze her vocal cords. 'Would you have done it?'

No hesitation. 'Without a doubt.'

'Shopped your own mother to the police?' she asked, disbelieving.

'Reb...' His eyes closed briefly, lips tightening. 'Miss Foley... My relationship with my mother is complicated.'

'It seemed perfectly normal from what I saw of it.' Well, relatively normal. Enzo and Silvana's world was so different to Rebecca's that it was impossible to judge their relationship by her own experiences. When Rebecca had returned home for weekends and holidays in her university years, her father had always collected her in the ancient family hatchback. For Enzo and Silvana, it was normal to visit each other via helicopter if traffic was particularly bad. Not that they drove themselves in any traffic, each having drivers on rotas to chauffeur them wherever they wanted to go. Then there was the nature of the visits. When back home, Rebecca and her parents had mucked in together with the cooking and cleaning as they'd always done. Enzo and Silvana each employed a fleet of domestic staff to prepare their meals and wipe away any dust before it dared land on their highly polished surfaces. There was also a heap of formality between Enzo and his mother as opposed to the affection and gentle teasing Rebecca and her parents had enjoyed, but in the formal settings of their respective homes, it had seemed natural.

'Appearances can be deceiving,' he said.

*You're the expert in that.* The words jumped to the tip of Rebecca's tongue but she pressed her lips together to stop the dig from escaping. It was the blaze from Enzo's eyes that did it. Fire and ice.

'Let me explain something to you.' Every word was delivered with bite. 'My mother never wanted to marry or have children. I was not planned. I was an accident. She handed me to my father when I was born because she did not want me.'

It wasn't just Rebecca's throat that froze at this. Every cell in her body turned to ice.

Not once in all their many talks had Enzo confided this to her. Not a hint of it.

'For the first six years of my life, my mother was nothing but an occasional visitor to our home. I barely knew her.'

'Then… How…?' She closed her mouth, unable to articulate a single one of the dozen questions swarming in her head.

'She did not want me or want to love me but, as she has told me many times since, she had no choice in the matter. She never wanted to have any involvement in my life but her love for me was stronger than her selfishness, and let me tell you, she hated it. To her, love stifles freedom. When my father died that love compelled her to claim me and take me in.' He let out a grunt and added, 'The day after my father's funeral, she collected me and that was it. The world I knew was gone and I had to live with this woman who was almost a stranger to me.'

Her heart throbbed, lungs aching for breath.

'If I'd been given the choice I would have

lived with my grandparents. They lived on the same street as us. I had always treated their home like my own. I loved them and they loved me. But I was six and not given a choice.'

Given a choice, Rebecca would have ripped her gaze away from him but her eyes refused to obey, soaking in the stony features, her fingers now gripping the spoon to stop them reaching across and stroking the hard edges away. This hardness was a side to Enzo she had never seen before and for reasons she would never understand affected her far more deeply than if he'd been relaying everything in a *pity me* voice.

She knew in her guts that everything he was telling her now was the unvarnished truth.

She'd known his father had died when he was six, known his parents weren't together when the aneurysm killed him, but had thought he'd always been raised by his mother.

Had she assumed that or had Enzo led her to believe it?

He'd deliberately let her make that assumption she realised dimly, because to have told her the truth would have been to open the can of worms that would have revealed his mother's true nature. As he'd already admitted, he hadn't wanted Rebecca to have any doubts about marrying him. He'd wanted nothing to make her believe he was anything less than perfect.

This time, though, she couldn't summon the energy to be angry about the revealing of yet another manipulative lie, not when she felt so sick inside for the little boy he'd once been.

Swallowing back bile, she forced herself to ask, 'What kind of mother was she once you were living with her?'

'Terrible,' he said bluntly. 'She is the most selfish person I know and had no idea how to raise a child. I went from a typical Italian life with a big extended family to living in an apartment where I was forbidden from touching anything. She resented me for cramping her style and I resented her for taking me away from my family and for not being my father.'

'What was your father like?'

There was a slight softening in his eyes. 'He was a great man. He worked as a painter and decorator. He painted cars all over the walls of my room for me. I have nothing but good memories of him.'

Another pang rippled through her chest. Words of comfort itched to jump off her tongue but she clamped them tightly, knowing she mustn't say them, that it was no longer her place to say them. That she shouldn't even want to.

Even if she felt she could, the look in Enzo's eyes told her comfort was neither wanted nor needed, that his past was something he'd already come to terms with and that he was only telling her the unvarnished truth because he owed it to her.

'Living with my mother...' He raised a shoulder. 'Neither of us liked the situation but there was no choice in it for either of us.' He shrugged again and drained his wine. 'She had no choice in loving me and I had no choice in loving her. Her love for me is the only reason we still have a relationship. She either likes people or she doesn't. If she likes you then she will do anything for you. Cross her and she will discard you as if you never existed. She is unable to discard me and that infuriates her. The threats I made to force her into becoming a law-abiding citizen would have seen anyone else cut from her life. I am quite sure she wishes she could cut me off but she can't, and she has spent five years seething with resentment. She saw the opportunity to strike at me and hurt me, and no doubt sated her conscience by telling herself she was doing it for your benefit.'

'Robina Hood has a conscience?'

Immediately she regretted her effort to lighten the oppressive atmosphere when a glimmer of humour passed between them.

She didn't want to be reminded of all the other glimmers that had passed between them because then it would lead to her remembering all the laughter and the sheer joy of just being with Enzo.

'I told you—her morality is complicated,' he said. 'If she had disliked you then I am certain she would have let you marry me and waited for a different opportunity to take her revenge.'

'Did she get some kind of kick out of being a criminal mastermind?' What other reason could there be for being so full of resentment?

'Undoubtedly.'

Rebecca stirred her spoon some more around her mostly uneaten meal and tried to square the Silvana Beresi she knew with the woman Enzo had just described, trying again to muster anger that in all the months they'd been together she'd bared her soul to him like she'd never done with anyone before while he'd blatantly omitted the most important aspects of his history to her.

He'd given her the skeleton of his life but failed, deliberately, to add flesh and blood to it.

But anger still refused to rise. Her heart continued to ache for the small boy he'd been, a child the same age as the children she taught. Those children were spontaneous in their affections and open with their emotions but not yet mature enough to hide whatever they were feeling. It was those who could hide it, she'd learned in the short time frame she'd been doing the job, that you needed to worry about. Would Enzo have been one of those children she'd watched closely, longing to hug them tightly and tell them everything would be all right?

Whatever kind of child Enzo had been, he was not that small boy any more. He'd grown into a man every bit as manipulative as the woman who'd given birth to him. He'd omitted the most important aspects of his life because he hadn't wanted to shatter the illusion of perfection and thus risk Rebecca having doubts about marrying him.

But she only knew this because he'd admitted it.

Now that everything was out in the open, he was giving her the honesty she demanded, and it made her heart hurt to think that if only he'd been honest with her from the start about her grandfather's will, maybe they…

There was no point in thinking like this. There was no *they*. Enzo didn't love her. He'd never loved her. Robina Hood had done her a huge favour.

Rebecca took a deep breath then pushed her chair back and got to her feet.

She sensed him watching her every move.

'It's late,' she said, turning her body away from him, too full of emotions she no longer understood to dare looking at him any more. 'I'm going to try and get some sleep.'

There was another painful clenching in her heart to remember that she should already be in bed. With her husband. Making love for the first time. Celebrating a love that had never existed.

His velvet voice drifted to her ears. 'Stay a little longer. I have something for you.'

She closed her eyes. 'The shares?'

'No. Something else.'

'There is nothing else that I want from you.' Other than for time to be reversed five months and to refuse a hot drink by the hotel fire with the most gorgeous man she'd ever set eyes on.

Too heartsick to breathe the same air as him a moment longer, Rebecca headed for the dining room door.

'Five minutes, *cara*. Stay with me until the clock strikes midnight.'

She stilled, closing her eyes again as fresh longing swept through her. 'You don't have a clock that strikes anything.'

'I was trying to be poetic.'

Despite herself, she smiled. Only a small smile but she was glad her back was to him and he couldn't see it. He shouldn't be able to amuse her still. She wished he didn't.

Footsteps sounded behind her. 'If we go now, we will be in the garage when midnight strikes.'

'Why the garage?'

'It's where your birthday surprise is.'

She shook her head violently. 'I don't want anything from you. Whatever you got for me, send it back.'

'That is not possible.'

The roots of her hair tingled at the warmth of his breath swirling through it. He was so close that every atom in her Enzo-starved body leapt towards his heat, and as she clenched her hands into fists to fight her yearning, she instinctively knew he was fighting the impulse to put his hands on the top of her arms and slide them down and then...

She started walking again, through to the main living room, fighting with everything she had not to look back. To look at him now, to find herself captured in the eyes that always pierced her soul, would drive her to madness.

'Okay, I'll have a look at your surprise.' She was thankful for the defiance in her voice. 'But don't expect me to be all gushing and grateful for whatever it is.' Undoubtedly a car. Enzo was a collector. His garage, filled with dozens of gleaming supercars that each cost more than her English home, had a larger footprint than her English home multiplied three times. Thankfully, Rebecca had no interest in cars. Her attachment to her father's old car that had led her into putting it into storage rather than selling it or, as she should really have been done, scrapping it, was purely emotional. Whatever car Enzo had bought her would have no emotional impact, and it surprised her that a man who'd proven himself so intuitive to her emotional needs—intuitive enough to manipulate her, she quickly reminded herself—would think otherwise.

Still not looking back, she crossed the vast room to the corridor and headed to the far end and through the door that opened into the stairwell and led down to the garage. Absolutely no way would she dare risk sharing the elevator with him.

Only the tread of Enzo's steps in her wake let her know he was behind her. That and the buzz in her veins and the pounding in her chest; the hyperawareness of his closeness she had once revelled in.

She quickened her pace down the stairs and stepped into the sprawling whitewashed underground lair that was as much a garage as a bed-sit was a mansion.

Folding her arms across her chest, Rebecca craned her neck in all directions. She would give her birthday car a cursory glance and then she would lock herself in the bedroom she'd never expected to sleep in again and take as cold a shower as she could stand and freeze all the dreadful heated feelings zipping through her veins and pounding in her heart.

In the third row to her left she caught the glimpse of a giant red bow. 'Is that it?'

'Yes. Come and see.'

It was only when she'd weaved through the second row and caught a glimpse of yellow that her heart lurched up into her mouth.

On legs that suddenly felt made of water, she virtually staggered to the vehicle she'd covered with a blanket only three weeks ago with the promise that she wasn't abandoning it and that when the time was right, she would take it out of storage and find someone to finish her father's restoration of it.

It took a long, long time for her to be able to speak and even then all she could muster was a choked, 'How?'

'I think you know the answer to that,' Enzo murmured before digging into his jeans pocket and pulling out a key. He held it out to her on his palm. 'Happy birthday, *cara.*'

She dragged her stare away from the car, and locked eyes with the man who'd made good on her father's dream.

The faded, battered vintage car that had so recently possessed so many dents it was impossible to count them all was now as smooth as the other cars in the showroom garage and gleamed with the same intensity, the ripped and stained upholstery now a richly textured leather... Nothing had been missed. Even the steering wheel and gear stick looked brand-new. And yet, it retained the original charm her father had fallen in love with. It was still the same car that had thrilled him so and which he'd been determined to wind the clock back on and restore to its former glory.

If her dad could see it now his face would be alight with that snaggle-toothed grin Rebecca missed so much.

The tears spilled out unbidden, and before she could stop herself, she ignored Enzo's outstretched hand to throw her arms around him and sob into his chest.

There was only the briefest hesitation before he wrapped his arms around her. One arm tight around her back, a hand cradling her head, his chin resting on her hair, he did nothing but hold her close, tenderly, wordlessly letting her purge the deluge of emotions she'd fought so hard to contain.

By the time her chest stopped heaving and the tears slowed to a trickle, his T-shirt was soaked.

She lifted her face. There was a tightness

to Enzo's features, different to the hardness from the dining room, as if he'd had to clamp the muscles of his face to stop himself from speaking.

'Thank you,' she whispered. The restoration of her father's car might only have been made possible due to Enzo's limitless funds but he'd thought to make it happen. For her. Because he knew how much it meant to her.

He gave a taut smile. 'I didn't mean to make you cry.' And then he winced as if remembering that he'd already made her cry an ocean of tears that long, long day.

'You didn't.' She swallowed to clear her throat. 'I'm just really feeling it today. Missing them.'

His face contorted into another wince. The fingers cradling her head threaded through her hair, the thumb from his other hand brushing away the dampness beneath her eyes. 'That's my fault.'

She couldn't argue with that. But she wanted to. Wanted to excuse him. Forgive him. Move her face the few inches needed for their lips to fuse together and find the dizzying joy his deep, passionate kisses always filled her with. Let him break her heart again.

And from the pulsing in his eyes, Enzo was fighting the same temptation too.

Breaking out of his hold, she stepped back, straight into the side of one of his Porsches.

But she couldn't break the fusion of their eyes. Couldn't tear her gaze from his.

And neither could he tear his gaze from her.

Eyes still holding hers, he dropped to his knees. She didn't know he'd dropped the key until he picked it off the ground and pressed it into her hand. His touch sent shocks of electricity darting through her skin.

The lock of their eyes somehow even stronger, hot, dark desire swirling in his, Enzo closed her fingers around the key. She could hear the shortness of his breaths. It matched the shortness of hers. The only other sound was the roar of blood in her ears, a roar that deafened when fingers gripped her hip as he rose, and hot breath danced over her mouth before she closed her eyes.

# CHAPTER SEVEN

REBECCA NEVER NEEDED to muster any resistance because the kiss never happened. Enzo's lips barely brushed against hers before he shot back as if he'd actually been shot.

He blew out a long breath and gripped a hank of his hair. 'I apologise,' he said stiffly.

Rebecca covered her flaming cheeks, mortified that he'd been the one to stop their kiss before it had even started. She'd been too far gone to stop it. Too caught in his spell.

It destroyed her that despite everything, her need for him was as strong as it had ever been whereas his control was a tap he could turn on and off at will.

He must have read something of what she was thinking on her face because suddenly he closed the gap he'd just made between them. His hands cradled her face roughly, his breath once again hot on her face. 'Do not think like this, *cara*,' he said savagely, then caught her hand, dragging it down his hard chest and abdomen and pressing it between his legs. 'Feel that and tell me I don't want you.'

Her breath hitched, eyes widening at the thick hardness straining against the denim of his jeans. A low, heady thrill rushed through her making her already watery legs weaken at the knees.

'I want you more than I have ever wanted anyone and I would give anything...' His nostrils flared. '*Anything* to make you mine. But I will not manipulate your emotions to my advantage. I will not be that man again.'

And then he released her completely and walked away.

Rebecca, still backed against the Porsche, stared at his retreating form, in too deep a stupor to even move her feet let alone comprehend what he'd just said.

Moments later, he disappeared into the elevator.

Rebecca brushed her teeth as hard as she could to scrub the taste of her own desire from her mouth. She'd taken another shower to wash the fever from her skin but all her efforts to sanitise herself against Enzo were fruitless. Every time she closed her eyes she felt his hardness against her hand. Every time, the pulse between her legs throbbed in response.

The purge of her tears had catharized everything except her desire.

How could she still ache so badly for him? After everything he'd done? So he'd done one good thing with the restoration of her father's car? That didn't change anything else or excuse him.

But he had done it. For her.

Telling herself to get a grip, she rootled through her wash bag for her moisturiser but came up empty. With a vague recollection of leaving it in the bathroom of the hotel room, she slipped back into the bedroom hoping one of the hotel staff had noticed and popped it in her case.

Her hope was fulfilled but as she wrapped her fingers around the cold jar, the side of her hand brushed against silk and her stomach turned over.

Gathering all her courage, Rebecca pulled the white negligée from the case and shook it out.

Her eyes swam. Memories of the dreams that had sustained her for so long flooded her.

This was what she'd planned to wear for Enzo on their wedding night. This night. In their honeymoon penthouse suite. All the possessions within the case open before her should have been moved to the suite in anticipation.

She'd planned it all out in her head, from the shower she'd take using the beautiful, sensuous shower gel she'd bought especially for this night, to the tempting makeup she would paint her face with. She hadn't wanted her first time to be all about her virginity. She had wanted it to be for the both of them. She had dreamed of Enzo's touch on every inch of her skin and dreamed of touching every inch of him too. In her dreams, their wedding night would *be* from the realm of dreams. Enzo's refusal to make love before their nuptials had only fed this fantasy.

And he would have made love to her that night. He would never have risked an annulment.

Almost unthinking, Rebecca took her pyjamas off and replaced them with the negligée she'd bought with her final monthly salary payment. She'd wanted to pay for it with her own money; her gift to the man she worshipped.

She stood in front of the mirror just as she'd done when she'd first bought it and had imagined the desire in Enzo's eyes before he stripped it from her.

The flattering cut made her look curvier than she actually was even if it didn't enhance her small breasts. Its spaghetti straps joined with the main body of silk, which skimmed her cleavage in a plunging V. The hem barely skimmed her bottom. This was not an item intended to be slept in. This was an item to be shared and enjoyed.

Still staring hard at her makeup-free reflection, Rebecca cupped her breast and imagined it was Enzo's hand caressing it. Closing her eyes, she imagined him replacing his hand with his mouth, and when her other hand slipped between her legs and brushed herself, a swell of rage burst through her and she wrenched her hands away from her hypersensitive zones and threw herself onto the bed she was never supposed to have slept in again.

It wasn't just her dreams for their wedding night Enzo had fed but the sickness raging in her blood—and there was no doubt her desire for him had morphed into a sickness, or else how could she be feeling so sick with desire for him now? His promise that the wait would all be worth it had set up in her mind impossibly unrealistic expectations and built what should have been perfectly ordinary desire into a fever that would never now be realised.

Was all this a punishment for being some kind of heinous person in a previous life?

Would she be feeling such heightened emotions for the man who'd broken her heart if she'd had previous experience of men? Would she be lying with her face buried in a pillow stifling screams if she'd already known another man's touch?

She couldn't kid herself that she wouldn't have fallen in lust with Enzo even if there had been men before him, but would she have been suckered in so completely? Would she be going through such agony now?

If only she'd found someone she felt strongly enough for to take the plunge and sleep with before her parents died then maybe she would have been better armed to spot the lie of his feelings and intentions from the beginning, but it had never happened. Her experience with men before Enzo had been practically nil. His good humour, charm, glamour and looks had dazzled her. Blinded her.

But she *had* continually asked questions, she argued with herself, angrily thumping the pillow for emphasis. Right from the start. Asked herself why a man like Enzo could fall for an ordinary woman like her.

She'd never questioned her own feelings though. Those she'd accepted from the beginning. She'd *welcomed* them, revelled in them because for the first time in so, so long, she was experiencing an emotion that wasn't grief.

Rebecca's natural shyness meant she'd always been most comfortable blended in a pack, the girls she hung around with her entire school life a middling gang who stuck together and went mostly unnoticed by their peers. When she got to university, she'd made new friends in her halls of residence. Unlike her old sedate school friends, these girls were wild—in comparison in any case—and dragged her out partying. She'd enjoyed it enormously but had been shocked with the ease some of her fellow students were happy to swap bodily fluids with people whose names they'd struggled to remember in the morning. She hadn't wanted her first sexual experience to be a drunken one-night stand. She'd wanted it to mean something. By her third year, her wild peers began to settle as the reality of the approaching big wide world loomed in their minds and made them knuckle down and actually do some work, but any hope Rebecca had of finding someone was forgotten when her mother's constant exhaustion was finally diagnosed as blood cancer. Two weeks later she was dead. Three days later, her shattered father suffered his fatal heart attack. In hardly the time it took to blink, Rebecca's world fell apart and she was plunged into a grief so complete it took her a full year to resume her studies.

The shell she'd hidden herself in had coated her until that cold, grey winter afternoon when Enzo had changed the tyre she now knew he'd punctured himself and bathed her world in colour.

He'd pulled her out of the fog of grief, brought her back to life and turned on the tap of her desire. But it had all been a lie and now she would never know what it felt like to give herself fully to a man and this awful fever would never be purged…

She pulled her face out of the pillow and shot upright, her heart thumping wildly.

This was all Enzo's fault. Everything. All those damn promises about their wedding night. He'd built this fever up in her.

Before she could change her mind, she scrambled off the bed and stormed out of the room, the fury driving her to Enzo's bedroom as alive in her veins as the desire.

Knocking loudly on his door, she didn't wait for an answer before shoving it open.

The curtains were open, the silvery light from the moon and stars pouring through the three windows enough for her to see. At the far end, in what she was convinced was the biggest bed in the world but one she'd been forbidden from sleeping in until they were legally husband and wife, Enzo lifted his head.

'Rebecca?' There was no sleepiness in his voice.

'Miss Foley to you,' she corrected angrily, kicking the door shut with her heel and crossing the vast floor space to him.

'What's wrong?' he asked, sitting up. The bed sheets slipped down to his waist revealing his bare chest.

The pulse between her legs throbbed with the same rage as the fury in her veins. All these months she'd fantasised about the moment she saw him undressed for the first time and the muscularity of his chest and the light smattering of dark hair covering it was so much more than her imagination had conjured. It only fuelled her anger; that she should be seeing it now, like this and not in the dreamlike state she'd so anticipated. That the power he held over her was stronger than it had ever been increased it to fever pitch.

It was time to claim that power for her own. She had let Enzo dictate everything for long enough. No more. Never again.

'I want the wedding night you promised me.'

He stared at her for a long moment before breathing deeply, leaning back against the headboard and closing his eyes.

'Don't close your eyes to me,' she snarled.

Jaw clenched, he fixed them on her face. 'You shouldn't be here.'

Ignoring him, she pulled at the straps of her bridal negligée. 'I bought this for you. For our wedding night. You were supposed to strip it off me with your teeth.'

His breathing became erratic. The throat she'd adored nuzzling moved convulsively. 'Go back to your room, Miss Foley.'

'I thought you wanted me,' she flared, climbing onto the bed. 'Or was that just another lie after all?'

He shook his head with ragged movements.

'Do you want me or not?' she demanded, straddling his lap. 'Is your desire for me a truth or a lie?'

His voice was thick. Pained. 'You know it's the truth.'

'Do I?' Grabbing the hem of her negligée, she whipped it over her head and threw it to one side. Something dark and angry had taken possession of her and she was glad of it, welcomed the fury firing through her veins. 'Then prove it.'

She would never have a wedding night. Not now. When Rebecca left this villa, that would be it for her. There was not a chance in hell that she would let another man get close enough to lay a finger on her.

Even if she ever felt she could risk it, she knew in her heart it would be pointless. No man could make her feel an ounce of what Enzo made her feel, and she *hated* him for it. Hated that he'd destroyed any chance of her forging a truly loving relationship.

He'd ruined her. For everyone but himself.

Enzo's eyes had darkened, his face taut, chest rising sharply. Not taking her eyes from his, she rested her hands on his naked chest for the first time and rubbed her fingers over the dark hair lightly covering it.

He sucked in a breath and shuddered. Somehow his eyes darkened further. Became hooded.

The pulse between her legs was throbbing stronger than ever, mingling with the sickness for him and her furious desire.

Suddenly he straightened from his recline against the headboard, hooking an arm around her back to stop her from losing her balance. His other hand cradled the back of her head.

'Who are you punishing here?' he asked in a thick undertone, long fingers spearing her hair, his face so close their lips were only a feather away from touching. 'You or me?'

The tips of her breasts brushed against his chest. The sensation was almost more than she could bear.

She cupped his cheeks and deliberately dug the pads of her fingers into the stubbly skin. 'Both of us,' she whispered harshly.

The grip on her hair tightened. The brown eyes boring into hers with such intensity were molten swirls. And then he groaned. In the breath of a moment, his lips fused to hers in a kiss so hard and passionate the pain of it was almost as acute as the pleasure.

Rebecca melted into it. Parting her lips in time with his, she dragged her fingers to the back of his head and clasped it as tightly as he clasped hers, the lock of their mouths deepening furiously, tongues plundering, teeth clashing.

She could have screamed her relief. This was what she wanted. What she needed. The hedonistic pleasure of Enzo's touch driving out the pain and obliterating her thoughts. She didn't want to think. For this one night, she just wanted to lose herself in Enzo.

Whatever was infecting her was clearly contagious.

Her breasts crushed against his chest, a strong hand swept feverishly over her naked back, over her shoulders, exploring her contours, dragging down her spine to the curve of her bottom and then sweeping back up again. The silk bed sheets were still across his lap, beneath it the full strength of his arousal hard against her mound, and it filled her with a burning heat to know that soon, finally, the wanton hunger so alive in her veins for him would be sated.

Breaking the lock of their mouths, he gazed at her. '*Mio Dio*, you're beautiful,' he muttered hoarsely before smothering her in another deeply passionate kiss that she felt all the way to the tips of her fingers and toes.

He'd been holding back she realised dimly when he wrenched his mouth from hers and pulled her head back, exposing her throat for him to devour. The fever she'd tasted in his kisses all those times before and the desire in his eyes had been mere shadows of what he was giving her now.

A hand slid beneath her bottom and raised her onto her knees before resting on the base of her spine, holding her steady as his lips and tongue caressed down to her breasts. The sensation that shot through her when he took one whole in his mouth made her cry out and wrap her arms around his neck. Pressing her mouth into the top of his head, she moaned at the intensity of it all. When the sensuous assault continued with her other breast, she barely noticed Enzo rip away the barrier of the sheets and lean her back until she was laid on the bed.

Only when he abandoned her breasts to

taste and explore the rest of her body did Rebecca learn how acute pleasure could really be, how it could arouse every cell until she became nothing but a receptacle writhing at an intimacy she'd spent months anticipating but which her imagination had utterly failed to do justice to. Frustrated desire had led her to explore her body alone many times since Enzo had come into her life but those briefly satisfying solo manipulations had in no way prepared her for the headiness of Enzo's face buried between her legs, his hands holding her waist tightly whilst he groaned in pleasure.

Any control she had over her own responses was lost when the thickening sensation building deep in her pelvis reached its pinnacle and exploded before she even realised it was going to happen. With a loud cry, her legs jerked involuntarily and her back arched as spasms of ecstasy ripped through her so powerful and consuming that only Enzo's hands gripping her waist stopped her from flying to the ceiling.

Slowly, the sensations lessened, all except the mad thrumming of her heart, and she became hazily aware of Enzo's mouth and tongue snaking their way back up her belly. She shivered as he licked her throat and then he was covering her entirely, his weighty erection jutting against the cradle of her thighs.

Opening her eyes, she gazed into his hooded stare and was hit by a tsunami of emotions.

The look in his eyes was everything she'd dreamed of seeing on her wedding night. Everything she was feeling, everything she was experiencing...

'I hate you,' she whispered raggedly when she was capable of drawing a breath.

His jaw clenched. 'I know.'

And then he kissed her with a savagery that stole her remaining breath.

Arms wrapped around his neck, she returned the kiss with equal fervour, all the love and all the hate she felt for him spilling out in an infusion of desire that pulsed deeply and was laced with an anticipation that made her heart beat even faster and harder.

This was it. The moment she'd spent so many long, lonely nights dreaming of.

He lifted his head.

The tips of their noses touching, his breathing uneven, he placed a hand on her thigh and gently spread it, then slid a hand beneath her bottom to raise it. All the while, the weight of his erection teased against her opening sending delicious, anticipatory heat flooding through her core.

Her whole body trembled.

She would swear his body trembled too.

He pressed his cheek against hers and then the thick, solid weight of his arousal slid into the place she ached the most for him to be, and her body opened like a flower.

With infinite care and tenderness, Enzo slowly, slowly filled her.

Rebecca's eyes were screwed shut. She was hardly breathing. Any pain was cocooned by the sensations flooding her. When their groins finally met, he placed his mouth to her cheek then brushed it over to her lips and kissed her with the same tenderness he'd taken possession of her.

'Hold on to me,' he murmured.

Closing her eyes even tighter, she tightened her hold around his neck and pressed her thighs closer against his.

Her heart raced so hard now it could be a hummingbird's wing.

With his hand still holding her bottom, he pulled out of her slowly, just a few inches, then drove slowly back to fuse their groins. And then he did it again, this time withdrawing a little further. When he drove back this time, the sensation made her gasp and her eyes fly open.

It was the concentration on his face that made her racing heart melt. He was holding back. Holding back because he didn't want to hurt her, and as she realised this, her lips found his and she wrapped her legs around him, suddenly needing them to be as close as it was humanly possible for two humans to be.

'Make love to me,' she whispered before clasping his head and deepening the kiss.

'*Mi amore*,' he groaned thickly into her mouth, his grip on her bottom tightening.

As the tempo of his lovemaking steadily increased, Rebecca was transported to a world of Enzo-induced bliss. Mouths locked together, she dragged her hands over his back, revelling in the smoothness of his hot skin, searching the contours and the bunching muscles, needing to touch him with a desperation she would never have believed possible, and all the while the pulses in her pelvis thickened as they'd done earlier, but this time with a completeness she hadn't even known had been missing, spreading through her burning veins, seeping down into her bones and up into her skin, drowning her in a sensation that crested to a peak and sent waves of the deepest, purest pleasure rippling through every part of her.

Arching her neck, she clung to him, crying out her ecstasy at the same moment Enzo called out her name and thrust into her so deeply and so completely that for one long, glorious moment, it felt like they were one and the same.

# CHAPTER EIGHT

WHEN THE RIPPLES of her climax subsided enough for Rebecca's head to clear, she squeezed her eyes shut and wished she could switch her brain off. Wished she could switch her senses off and not be inhaling Enzo's warm skin or have the taste of it pressed against her lips or have his slowly steadying breaths in her hair or feel the heavy thumps of his heart against her own. Wished she could bring herself to push him off her and stalk out of his room with the same brazen fury with which she'd entered it.

But the passionate fury that had driven her to his bed had evaporated and now she was left with the consequences of allowing the sickness that had infected her to override any sense she had.

She should have been less inhibited and joined in with the body fluid swapping her party-loving university friends had indulged in. She might have struggled to remember the names of the faces she woke beside but at least she wouldn't be holding on for dear life to stop hot tears from spilling at the monumental mistake she'd just made.

What she'd just experienced was more than in her wildest fantasies; not the things they'd done but the intensity of the feelings evoked in her. And, she suspected with a choked heart, evoked in Enzo.

But not the same ones. Whatever alchemy they'd just shared, for him it had been nothing but a chemical rush. When Rebecca left this villa, he would feel her absence only fleetingly. To miss someone, truly miss them, they had to have touched your soul. Enzo would not miss her. For him, this passion between them was nothing but a side effect of the game he'd been playing all these months.

The game had been played without Rebecca's knowledge, but it had been everything to her. He'd been everything to her.

He still was, and she had to swallow hard to stem the tears as the impossibility of her love punched through her with the strength of a heavyweight's blow.

Making love with him hadn't purged her of

anything. It had made everything worse, and now she had to double the strength needed to walk away as the emotions raging in her choked heart felt fit to burst. Because only now did it hit her, fully hit her, that it wasn't just the tools to mend her shattered heart she needed to find but the tools to navigate her life without him.

The only positive she could find to cling to was that her insanity wouldn't result in a pregnancy, but even that positive lasted only a flicker as it set off another pang of loss. Rebecca had gone on the pill a few months ago. They'd both agreed the first year of their marriage would be just for the two of them and then they'd start trying for a baby.

There would be no baby now. Not for them. Never for her. Not now.

Enzo slowly turned his face and kissed the top of her ear. 'Say something,' he murmured.

Unable to speak, she pressed her mouth even tighter into his neck and shook her head.

Carefully, he shifted his weight off her, rolling onto his back, taking her with him so she was cuddled onto him, her cheek on his upper chest, his chin resting on the top of her head.

One arm tight around her, he caught her hand and threaded their fingers together. 'Did I hurt you?'

She couldn't stop herself from squeezing his fingers. 'No.' Her voice was barely audible.

There had been no pain. Only bliss. Any pain in the aftermath was entirely her own fault.

He pressed his mouth into the top of her head and kept it there.

She wished he could keep it there for ever.

So many wishes. None of which could come true.

The silence stretched until he quietly said, 'Tell me what you're thinking.'

Her answer came without any thought. 'That my parents' marriage gave me completely unrealistic expectations.'

'What makes you think that?'

Rebecca laughed morosely and finally made herself move, slipping her hand out of his hold and using his chest as a lever to sit herself up. Somehow they'd managed to end up on the other side of the bed to the pillows. She was certain there was a kind of symbolism in this but was too heartsick to think what it could be.

The silk bedsheets were all unravelled and she pulled at them to cover herself, holding them across her breasts and shuffling so her back was to the pillows.

Now facing him, she met Enzo's stare and the longing that ripped through her to throw herself back on him and be held tightly to him, skin on skin, had her gripping the sheets with all her strength. 'Their marriage was happy.'

He hooked an arm behind his head as a prop, his magnificent, naked body stretching with the motion. It had been barely a minute since she'd moved away from him but already she felt bereft without the comfort of his touch, and, as hard as she tried, she couldn't stop herself from gazing at him.

'Is happiness in a marriage unrealistic?' he asked.

Less than a day ago she would have said no. What she'd felt in her heart and believed Enzo felt in his heart had convinced her a lifetime of happiness was theirs for the taking.

'The level of happiness they shared is.' She'd been a fool to think she could have it too. 'They were just so wrapped up in each other. Sometimes I felt like a third wheel.'

Not sure where this admission had come from, she leaned forwards and gripped her calves. 'Did my grandfather tell you he tried to pay my dad off?'

'Yes.'

That made her eyebrows rise. Who would actually admit doing something like that? 'Was he ashamed of that?'

'No. He never stopped believing your father was bad for your mother.'

Anger flared at the grandfather she'd never met but whom Enzo had known well enough for Ray Claflin to confide the most personal information to. Known and trusted.

'He was only bad for her if you don't believe women have free will,' she said with an attempt at tartness. 'Mum quit university because she couldn't bear to be parted from him. That was her choice but he blamed my father for it and he'd never even met him. He *refused* to meet him. He didn't know my father. He had no right to make that kind of judgement.'

'He came to accept that his attempts to drive them apart backfired and pushed them closer together.'

'I think that's pretty arrogant of him. If he'd given my father a chance instead of judging him as unworthy because he left school at sixteen and worked as a mechanic then he'd have seen my father adored my mum and would have done anything for her.'

Enzo didn't say anything, just looked at her, and another flare of anger burned to know he was remembering how she'd mentioned that her first visit to Florence to see him had been only her second trip abroad, the first being a school trip to France her parents had scrimped and saved to pay for. It always made her feel wretched to know they'd been so close to doing all the things they'd never been able to afford before. Their mortgage had nearly been paid off, Rebecca close to finishing her degree and becoming financially independent... They'd barely hit middle age. They'd assumed they had multiple decades left to explore the world.

'They might have struggled financially but I never went without and I always had emotional security. I never had a single fear that they would divorce. They were devoted to each other and just so affectionate...always having to touch each other. It was like they needed reassurance the other was there.'

She closed her eyes. Hadn't that been one of the things she'd so adored about Enzo?

His need to touch her? It had been as strong as her need to touch him. Had been one of the many things that had convinced her their marriage would be as strong and as happy as her parents' had been. And hadn't she quit her job to be with him just as her mum had quit her degree? All her life, she'd had a romantic, idealised vision of her parents' marriage…

'Cara?'

She blinked back into focus and looked at him. The concern in his stare made her heart clench. Looking away, she put her focus on her toes, painted a deep cherry red to match her nails. She'd never been one for bold colours before but there was something about being with Enzo that had made her feel bold. Seen…

'My expectations for our marriage were entirely unrealistic,' she whispered. 'All along I knew there was no way a man like you would look at a woman like me but you were so convincing. And then there was the fable I grew up with of my parents; of the rich girl from the right side of town falling for the poor boy on the wrong side of town, and it all worked in my mind to convince me that you and I were meant to be, but all along, what I was looking for was *their* marriage, to be the most important person in someone's life, to not...'

To not what? Rebecca hadn't meant to say any of that. Not consciously. The words had fallen off her tongue as she'd been thinking them, but now she'd hit a block and there was a heavy pulse beating in her brain. *To not what...?*

'To not be the one left behind?' he supplied quietly when her unspoken words remained unformed and unsaid.

Her heart punched her ribs and, completely thrown, her gaze shot back to him. 'Why would you say that?'

He sat up. His clear brown eyes shrewd, the outer part of his thigh pressed against hers, he took hold of her hand. 'Why did you feel like a third wheel?'

Rebecca had always thrilled at the muscularity of Enzo's masculine physique compared to the slender femininity of hers. With the moonlight pouring on them, she noticed properly for the first time the paleness of her skin set against his olive tone. A day ago, she would have marvelled at the contrast, *delighted* in it. Now, for reasons she could never begin to understand, it opened another fissure in her heart. 'It was just a saying.'

'You would not have said it if it didn't mean something. Did you feel that you were in the way?'

Cheeks burning, she shook her head vehemently. 'No. They loved me. I never doubted that.'

'But not as much as they loved each other?'

Her heart gave another punch, and she snatched her hand away. 'What a cruel thing to say.'

There was compassion laced in the steel of his stare. '*Cara*, I am trying to understand—'

'There is nothing to…' *understand,* she meant to add, but something like panic had thickened her throat too much for any more words to form.

'There is everything to understand,' he said, perfectly reading the train of thought she barely understood herself. Leaning his face into hers, close enough that Rebecca could see the flecks of gold swirling in the pupils, he pitched his tone low but with the same formidability as in his stare. 'If you could see into my heart and head, you would know the insecurities that made you question why a man like me would want a woman like you were without foundation—'

He'd said exactly the right thing to make her fight the panic. With a bark of ironic laughter, she interrupted him. 'Enzo, have you forgotten that I know exactly why a man like you wanted a woman like me? You set everything up between us so you could get your greedy mitts on my grandfather's business shares.'

'That only accounts for how things started, and if I hadn't been so afraid of losing you I would have told you the truth a long time ago.' He put a finger to her lips to stop her interrupting him again. The flecks of gold had turned into flames. 'I *know* it is over for us. I know that in a matter of hours you are going to leave my life for good and that nothing I say will stop that. I will not go against my word and tell you how that makes me feel but if you didn't have the insecurities that made you feel you're not good enough for me, I wouldn't need to tell you. You would already know. You would still have left me at the altar and wanted to punish me but you would never have doubted *me*. Those insecurities came from somewhere.'

She snatched the finger pressed at her lips,

but instead of shoving it aside, squeezed it. 'Nice try. If I was writing a school report, I would say you were imaginative but given to flights of fancy.'

His eyes narrowed. For a long moment he stared at her with the stillness of a statue.

With a cauldron of emotions bubbling and swirling so violently inside her, it took everything Rebecca had to maintain eye contact and keep her own features poker straight.

And then he gave a disbelieving smile and shook his head slightly. 'If you think I said that in the hope of changing your mind then you have just made my point for me. You, *cara*, are worth more to me than anything. I'd give you my own damn shares to make you believe that.'

Almost giddy with relief at the change of direction and being back on familiar territory, she smiled. If he wanted to play the game some more then fine. Better than him trying to dissect *her*. 'Go on then.'

His right eyebrow shot up. 'You want the whole business?'

'Not particularly. I wouldn't know what to do with it, but you're welcome to give it all to me and see if that makes me believe you magically developed feelings for me beyond lust.' This was better. Now she felt in control of herself. The pulse in her brain had quietened to a low beat, the panic lessened to a thrum.

A gleam came into his eyes, lighting his whole face with a lascivious magnetism that sent liquid pooling deep in her pelvis where the aftereffects of their lovemaking still gently buzzed.

Dropping his voice and leaning his face even closer to hers, he murmured sensuously, 'Ah, so you believe now that I wasn't faking my desire for you?'

The liquid contracted into a throb. Loosening her hold on his finger to spear their hands together, she had to swallow the moisture that had suddenly filled her mouth to speak. 'You proved that very well, thank you, and if you want to prove all the things you spouted about how your feelings and stuff were true by giving me all of Claflin Diamonds then feel free. Maybe I'll turn into a business mogul…or maybe I'll give the whole thing to the dog charity I mentioned earlier.'

The fingers threaded through hers tightened, the gleam in his eyes deepening. 'Marry me and I'll sign all of my business interests over to you and you can do your worst with the lot of it.'

Thick thrills of desire racing through her blood, Rebecca inched her face even closer. 'Throw in the New York apartment and the jet, and I'll think about it.'

His face tilted, his gaze drifting to her mouth. 'You can have it all. Everything.'

Arousal had built so thoroughly in her that she could hardly speak. 'Either you're desperate for those shares or you really do think I'm an idiot.'

'No, *cara*, just desperate to keep you in my life.' His lips caressed hers.

She was completely unable to stop a moan escaping. Staring into his eyes was like gazing into a dark pool of lust and she knew he was seeing the same from her own stare. Her words when they came were a breathless whisper. 'Think I'm going to have to add to your school report, "Enzo tries too hard."'

He pulled her hand down to his abdomen where his arousal stood to attention. '*This* is the only thing that's too hard.'

Her eyes widened and she instinctively wrapped her fingers around the long, thick velvet. Fresh moisture filled her mouth as it throbbed and strained at her touch.

He shuddered and clasped her hip. 'This is what you do to me,' he said hoarsely. 'You can't deny this. This is all you.' And then he parted her lips with his tongue and delved deep into her mouth.

There was no more conversation.

When Rebecca awoke, the room was still in darkness. Beside her, face turned to hers, his hand heavy on her stomach, lay Enzo. From the heaviness of his breathing, he was deep in sleep. Her own sleep had been brief, a snatch of slumber brought about by her body's exhaustion but which turned out to be no match for her overloaded brain. She didn't need to look at her watch to know she'd had no more than an hour of oblivion.

She tried to take her own heavy breath to stop the prickling of tears releasing but the compression in her chest was too much. She needed air. Needed to escape this bed before the thoughts in her head and the emotions churning in her took control again.

Still trying desperately to breathe, she crept out of bed, pulled her discarded negligée over her head and quietly left the room. In the corridor she wiped the tears away and put her hand to her thrashing heart, and managed to drag a tiny amount of air into her tight airways before staggering to the room she should have slept in.

The bed she would have slept in if she hadn't allowed her emotions to take control was still rumpled from where she'd thrown herself on it in a fit of frustrated pique. Her suitcase was still open, half the contents spilled messily around it.

Rubbing at another leaking tear, she pulled her robe out of the suitcase and slipped it on, tightening it around skin still tender and alive from Enzo's passionate lovemaking. Just to think about that made her legs weaken.

God help her, it had been the best night of her life.

And the worst.

Self-recriminations were pointless. She'd known what she was doing, going to his bed.

But she'd never dreamed how good it would be. Not that *good* carried a fraction of the meaning of what it had been like. The dizzying heights he'd taken her to, again and again. The sheer exhilarating headiness of it all. If she could switch her heart off she'd be tempted to move all her stuff to his room right now, straddle him awake and demand he be her sex slave for as long as it took to slake the passion between them. Just to imagine his response to this demand made her core throb with an arousal she could hardly believe hadn't been spent through the hours they'd passed with their limbs wrapped around each other.

But her heart could not be switched off. Each kiss, each caress, each climax, it had all pushed her further over the line of being hopelessly in love, and it was a love that would never be reciprocated. It couldn't be. Not from him.

All these thoughts were pointless. She needed to pull herself together and stop wishing for things that could never be.

Padding quietly down to the kitchen, she didn't even consider pressing an intercom to wake the duty member of staff to fix a drink for her. Turning the switch by the door, she blinked away the effect of the bright lights assaulting her unadjusted eyes and headed straight to the cupboard that contained the coffee. She pressed the cupboard door open and her heart jumped.

Blinking again, she reached for the rectangular box neatly placed next to the large bag of coffee beans. It was no trick of the light, and in an instant she was transported back to the very beginning when she'd accompanied the gorgeous Italian who'd selflessly changed her flat tyre into the hotel. She'd been giddy at the thought of spending an hour in his company; a spring in her step and a zest in her veins she'd never felt before. It was when Enzo had steered her past the bar to a table that she'd spotted the clear jars filled with the distinctive triangular teabags of her favourite brand in a neat row beside the barista machine. Her thoughts of having a hot chocolate had been immediately abandoned. At least five times the price of her usual tea, this was the brand she treated herself to a packet of each year for her birthday, something she had a dim recollection of telling Enzo when they gave their order. She'd been utterly thrilled to see it on the bar's shelf, and as she'd sat there sipping it, eyes glued to Enzo's face, she had wondered if her day could get any better.

He'd remembered, she realised, her head swimming. He must have done. She'd never even mentioned tea since that day—well, who in their right mind discussed *tea*?—but she knew it hadn't been in the cupboard three days ago, the last time she'd fixed herself a drink here.

Enzo had bought it for her as a birthday surprise.

# CHAPTER NINE

STILL DAZED AT the teabag find, Rebecca carried her mug up to the roof terrace, a sprawling area with a swimming pool and seating dotted around its perimeter. The last time she'd come up here it had been in the dead of night with Enzo, when romantic solar-powered lights had guided their way. That early morning, a glimmer of orange lined the horizon. The sun was waking up.

Inhaling the sweetly scented air of the climbing flowers around the perimeter wall, she peered out of the section that overlooked the front of Enzo's grounds. Looking hard, she could make out the shadows of the reporters still camped on the other side of the electric gate and her heart sank. Barely half a day ago she'd been fully prepared to give them all the ammunition they needed to destroy Enzo. But that was before. Before she'd found paradise in his arms.

She could no more destroy him than she could kick a puppy.

To stay though, would be to destroy herself.

Enzo's villa was located on the top of a hill with some of the best views money could buy. Curled up on a white sofa on the other side of the terrace, she watched the sun rise over a sleeping Florence.

The morning after he'd proposed, Enzo had woken her early and insisted she join him in this exact spot to enjoy this exact view. He'd watched her reaction, his dimples prominent.

He'd wanted to share it with her. He'd wanted her to love the sunrise as much as he did.

Suddenly unable to bear the memories the beautiful sunrise was evoking, Rebecca pulled her phone out of her robe pocket and, in desperate need of distraction, finally turned it on.

She'd guessed there would be numerous messages left on it but had massively underestimated. Messages from names she'd hardly thought of in years were interspersed with family, friends and recent colleagues. All the messages were a variant of the same theme.

What's happened?

Are you okay?

Please let me know you're okay.

Call me.

Let me know you're safe.

Taking a deep breath first, she got busy replying, prioritising her aunt and cousins.

I'm fine, I promise. Will explain everything when I see you.

Would she really? Could she really do that? Explain that the great love of her life and the romantic story it had been based upon had all been a lie? Put Enzo at risk of someone sensing a way to make themselves some money and tip a reporter off?

She almost laughed. She was worried about putting him at risk? Seriously, someone needed to give her a martyr's badge or something. She wasn't going to lie for him. He'd made his bed. He didn't need her protection. Besides, he could afford some swanky lawyers to suppress any rumours, she was sure. That's what rich people did when it came to stopping the exposure of stories with narratives they didn't like, wasn't it?

But there was nothing he could do to stop them reporting Rebecca's jilting of him at the altar, and before she could talk herself out of it, she keyed in the name of the UK's biggest selling tabloid.

Its homepage filled her screen. *Jewellery Magnate Jilted!* screamed the headline. Two photos lay beneath it. One was a distant, blurry image of Rebecca climbing onto the back of her saviour's Vespa. The other was a close-up of Enzo on the cathedral steps, his gaze fixed into the distance. Searching. Searching for *her*. His handsome features—and, God, didn't the camera just adore him—were tight, giving nothing away. But his eyes... They were wild. If she looked closely enough she could imagine she saw distress in them.

Unable to endure the image a second longer, Rebecca swiped the page away and sucked in a huge gulp of air.

What had she done?

Hold on a minute, what had *she* done? Was she really that desperate for a martyr's badge that she'd forgotten this was all on Enzo? If he'd told her the truth about her grandfather's will from the beginning then none of this would have happened and she'd never have gone to the cathedral in such an emotional state. And if she accepted that he'd been too angry at her grandfather's trick to want to discuss it with her—and he was right in that he hadn't known her back then—then why hadn't he paid his swanky lawyers to talk to her? Wasn't that what lawyers were paid to do? Overcome obstacles? But it had been the will itself that was the biggest obstacle so why not try to overturn it? His excuses on this score were only plausible when you weren't talking about a multibillionaire. Enzo could afford the finest legal team money could buy. She would have been no match for him.

Movement behind her cut her thoughts off in their tracks.

Twisting her head, her insides contracted as Enzo's messy dark brown hair appeared at the top of the stairs. The rest of him appeared in stages until he was stalking the terrace towards her wearing nothing but a pair of black swim shorts.

All the mornings they'd spent together and this was the first time she'd seen him not fully clothed. The first and the last.

Rebecca swallowed and smiled a greeting at the man she knew it would take every ounce of her strength to walk away from.

He gazed at her, nostrils pulling in at the deepness of his breath. And then his dimples flashed. 'Enjoying the view, Miss Foley?'

She let her gaze drift down to his chest, her heart swelling, pulses stirring. 'Very much.'

Eyes glittering, he sat himself on the chair beside hers, stretched his long legs out and looked out at the colourful city of his birth under the cloudless sky. 'All your grandfather's liquid assets have been transferred to you. The house is yours. The shares will be yours within hours. When the banks open tomorrow you will be rich enough to buy yourself a view anywhere you want.'

The anger that usually flared at the mention of the shares refused to rise. Whether it was the realisation that this, here, now, was the beginning of the end for them or because she could still see the tabloid headline and feel the tendrils of guilt at the scandal that had erupted about them, or because of the buzz in her veins to be sat next to a semi-naked Enzo; whatever the reason, the tempest in her chest had receded.

She didn't want to argue any more.

Rebecca lifted her face to the lightening sky and tried not to wish that this was the sky she woke to for the rest of her life. 'I'm not keeping any of it. Don't ask about the shares—I need time to think about what I'll do with them and I can't think straight when I'm sitting next to you, but I know I won't keep the rest of it.'

The Claflin Diamond shares were a quandary to be resolved when she was alone but whatever she did with them, she knew now that she would never use them as a weapon against Enzo. Even if he did deserve it.

He was quiet for a long time. 'I understand why you would want to reject it but do not make any hasty decisions.'

'He never told my mum my grandmother died. Did you know that? She only learned her own mother had died by chance—a friend of hers read the obituary. Can you imagine what that did to her?' Broke her mother's heart is what it did to her. 'How can I keep the money when it comes from someone who caused such pain?'

There was another long pause of silence. 'All I will say is that you're feeling raw. Do not make the same mistake as me and let betrayal and grief take you in a direction you come to regret. I know you found my world overwhelming at times but I also witnessed your happiness at seeing new countries and in all the new experiences we shared. Do you really want to go back to a world limited by suburbia?'

'It wasn't limited,' she disagreed.

'That is not what I observed from your reactions to my world. *Cara*, your parents felt it too. They had plans to travel. You told me. They were waiting for you to finish your degree and to pay off their mortgage.'

'Travelling was their dream, not mine.'

'That money will free you,' he told her bluntly.

'I already live mortgage-free.' The rent Rebecca currently received for her house would pay for her to rent somewhere until the tenancy ran out and she could move back in.

Such sad irony though, that her parents had to die to be free of all their debts, their insurance paying the remainder of their mortgage off, and as she thought this, she realised that, as when they'd talked about the shares, yesterday's pain had receded. She had a strong suspicion it wouldn't last but for now it was bearable. She would take that.

In the distance, breaking the early morning silence, a horn tooted. The sound reminded her of the way her Vespa boy saviour had tooted at pedestrians in lieu of running them over when she'd run from the cathedral.

She turned her face to Enzo and smiled. 'You stole a Vespa.'

His lips pulled into a grin. '*Sì*. I took the keys from the hand of a delivery boy.' He twisted in his chair and leaned into her to rub a finger over the rim of her ear. 'You have made a criminal of me.'

She arched a brow, shivering at the pleasure of his light tough. 'Made a criminal of you? Are we really going to go there?'

He shook his head and threaded his fingers through her hair. 'I have already made contact with him and transferred the value of the Vespa with extra for the inconvenience.' Something sparked in his stare and for a moment he gazed intently at her before his dimples reappeared. 'Shall we go for a ride?'

'A ride?' she echoed.

'The Vespa is now mine. Let's take it for a ride. Enjoy the morning before the sun gets too hot for your delicate English skin to cope with.'

His teasing made her mouth smile and her heart twist. There had always been so much teasing between them. In seven hours or so, there would be no more. They would never tease each other again.

'What about the press?'

His dimples deepened and he lowered his face to whisper in her ear, hand slipping through the gap in her robe to grip her hip. 'There is a secret route off my land.'

His touch and breath on her skin provoked another, deeper shiver of pleasure, and Rebecca did the only thing that made sense and closed the small distance between them so her breasts were flush with his chest, and turned her face so their mouths brushed together. 'You've never mentioned it,' she murmured, arousal turning her veins to hot, thick treacle.

Teeth tugged gently at her bottom lip in complete contrast to the delicious pain of his fingers digging harder into her hips before splaying down to her bottom and diving beneath the silk negligée to clasp a bare buttock.

'That's because a car cannot travel it.' His voice was hoarse. Ragged. His other hand stole around to the small of her back then drifted lower to hold her other buttock. 'A Vespa can.'

One moment she was on her chair, the next lifted off it and straddling Enzo's lap. His erection jutted hard through his shorts. She writhed against him and groped for the button of his shorts.

How was it possible to still feel such dizzying *need* for him after the night they'd just shared and with hardly any sleep?

A moment later, his erection was freed. The moment after that Rebecca stopped thinking at all.

Florence was on the cusp of waking up when Rebecca and Enzo escaped the villa. Those of its people not enjoying a Sunday morning lie-in would be opening their eyes to another beautiful summer's day. Rebecca doubted that anyone would appreciate it in the way she was determined to.

Only seven a.m. With only one hour of sleep, she should be shattered but there was a glow to her skin and in her heart that over-rode any exhaustion, and as they zipped through the lemon trees of Enzo's estate, her hands rested lightly on his hips and she lifted her face to the slowly rising sun, determined to make the most of these last six hours with him. It wasn't as if she could do any more harm to herself. She couldn't love him any more than she did. Leaving him couldn't hurt any more than it was going to do. The price to be paid would be the same if she spent the next six hours locked in a room away from him.

After a couple of minutes spent following the narrow trail, they reached a small gate in the perimeter wall. Enzo punched the code to open it and then they were riding on a dust track that soon connected to the main road the press was camped along. In moments, the press pack was far behind them, unaware their targets had evaded them.

The roads they travelled were mostly empty of traffic but the deeper they rode into the city, the more human life began to emerge, street cleaners sweeping away the night's litter, young parents with babies and toddlers in prams and strollers, dog walkers; all interspersed with the odd vampiric figure staggering back to their bed after a night of hard partying. Unlike the Vespa boys of the day before, Enzo rode at a sensible pace. Rebecca didn't doubt that if she hadn't been riding as his passenger, he'd be extracting every inch of speed he could out of it.

The scent of fresh coffee filled her nostrils and she wished she could remove the helmet and press her cheek into his back and close her eyes and fill her lungs with both Enzo's scent and the scent she would always associate with this beautiful city. Tempting though it was, he would go berserk if she removed it. They'd only the one helmet between them and he'd insisted she wear it, going as far as to put it on her himself and securing the strap. Oh, well, it wasn't as if he couldn't afford the fine that would be slapped on him if they got pulled over for Enzo's own failure to wear one.

After crossing the river, they entered a part of the city she'd never visited before. Soon they turned the corner near a vast piazza and entered a narrow street lined with all manner of grocery shops that, if it were not Sunday, would have cheeses, hams, fruits and vegetables displayed under the colourful awnings.

Enzo pulled over by—yippee!—an open

coffee shop with outdoor seating. After parking the Vespa next to two others, he helped Rebecca dismount then, with a smile, unclipped her helmet and pulled it off her head. Immediately she fluffed her hair up, making him grin at this little display of vanity and ruffle her hair, which in turn made her slap his hand.

'Pack it in,' she scolded, straightening her buttoned olive-green dress which fell to just above her knees.

His eyes sparkled. 'Make me.'

She gave him her best schoolteacher face, making his grin widen so much she could practically see all his straight white teeth.

He was still grinning once he'd taken his seat, his dimples flashing when a member of the waiting staff, eyes still puffy with sleep, came out to take their order. With a strange, almost manic energy fizzing inside her, Rebecca couldn't stop smiling either. She didn't think she'd ever felt the rays of the early morning sun so strongly before or experienced such awareness of her surroundings, as if all her senses had been injected with caffeine, making everything sharper, from the scent of Enzo's cologne to the smart khaki shorts and black T-shirt his beautiful body was wrapped in. The pigeons scavenging crumbs and the few people milling about were sharply in focus too, although she doubted any of them would think for a moment that the couple sitting al fresco at this ungodly time for a Sunday were at the top of the European press's most wanted list. And if they were recognised...well, they'd get back on the Vespa and Enzo would whisk them away.

Not until their breakfast had been brought out to them and the pastries demolished did Enzo put his phone down from reading a message he'd received, don his shades—the sun really was gaining strength and today promised to be a scorcher—nod at the five-storey faded yellow building that ran the length of the street on the other side of the road facing them, and idly say, 'That's where I lived with my father.'

Startled at this unexpected revelation, she tried to read his stare beneath the darkness of his shades before giving up and turning her attention to his early childhood home. 'Which apartment?'

'Directly opposite. Third floor above the pizzeria.'

She counted up to the Juliette balcony with potted plants showing between the rails.

'It was a greengrocer when I was a child,' he told her. 'The owner would give me an apple every morning when I walked to my grandparents'.'

The grandparents she'd never met.

'Which one was theirs?'

'First floor above the florist.' She found the balcony, one of many on the building with laundry drying on it. 'They had a communal garden I played in. It was only small but it had a slide and a swing that I would fight with the other children to play on.'

Rebecca closed her eyes and slowly filled her lungs, trying to hold on to the fizzing energy, trying to eradicate images of a small Enzo hurtling himself down a slide. Twenty-four hours ago she'd still been unaware that Enzo had spent the first six years of his life living with his father.

In a few short hours it would be exactly a day since his mother had thrown the grenade that had imploded her world. 'Why are you showing this to me?'

'Because I wanted you to see where I really come from before you leave. And because I owe it to my father. I should never have diminished his role in my life or the role my grandparents played in those early days. Another regret for me to live with.' He gave a quick, wry smile then sighed and looked back at his childhood home. 'I can still hear his voice and hear him telling me off for trying to climb onto the balcony railing and I can still smell the turpentine he used to clean his brushes, but his face disappeared a long time ago. I can spend an hour looking at a photograph trying to fix him back into my mind and then the next day he's gone again, and now I have to live with knowing I pushed him further away in my mind for my own ends. My grandparents too.' He grimaced. 'They asked many times to meet you before the wedding. I made all the excuses to them.'

'Couldn't risk them telling me the truth about your early years?'

'Yes.' This time she could see through the darkness of his shades to his eyes and the self-recrimination blazing from them. 'I saw little of them after I moved in with my mother but for the first six years of my life they were a huge fixture of my life. My grandmother collected me every day from school. She always cooked my favourite food for me—you think Sal makes a good *melan-*

*zane alla parmigiana* but no one makes it as good as her.'

It took a beat for Rebecca to realise he was talking about the aubergine and mozzarella dish he so loved.

'Like your family, my father and my grandparents struggled for money but I never went hungry or cold. What I remember most about the first six years of my life is being safe and happy.'

There was nothing Rebecca could say to this. As when discussing his mother's initial abandonment of him, everything Enzo was telling her was delivered matter-of-factly. Sympathy and platitudes were neither expected nor required.

He wouldn't want to hear it but it hurt her heart to think he'd only known safety and happiness for his first six years.

She had to respect that he could hold his hands out and admit to the wrongs he'd committed.

Finishing her cappuccino, she couldn't help but wonder how a man so clear-headed and principled—she could hardly believe she was thinking of Enzo and *principled* in the same sentence, but that's why she usually limited her caffeine intake—could go to the lengths Enzo had done. He didn't *need* Claflin Diamonds. With his fortune, he could have created a dozen brand-new fully staffed laboratories in every country on earth and still had change to spare.

Before she could find the question to probe, his lips quirked and he reached over and wiped her top lip.

'Cappuccino moustache,' he explained with a grin, then popped the finger used to wipe the froth away into his mouth.

Rebecca couldn't begin to explain why this one little gesture felt more intimate than all the things they'd done in bed together or why it made her chest ache so badly.

'Always the gentleman,' she said lightly.

'Always.' He held his hand out to her. 'Come, Miss Foley, I have one more place to show you.'

'Your mother's apartment when she first took you in?' she guessed.

He leaned across the table and kissed her. 'Didn't I say how smart you were?'

# CHAPTER TEN

TRAFFIC WAS DECIDEDLY heavier on the second leg of what had become a tour of Enzo's childhood, but still much lighter than during the working week and on Shopping Saturday. Although keeping to the safe speed he'd adopted on the first leg, Enzo nipped in and out of the traffic like a pro, and when he came to a stop outside an apartment building in a decidedly swankier district than the one he'd lived in until his father's death, this one screaming wealth in the same way his father's district had screamed family, the first thing Rebecca asked when he'd removed her helmet was, 'Have you had a Vespa before?'

His dimples popped and his teeth flashed. 'A Vespa was the first thing I bought when I turned eighteen.'

'You were a Vespa boy?'

'Much to my mother's disapproval.'

'Is that why you bought it?'

'Her disapproval was a plus but not the reason.'

'Girls?'

He tapped her nose and laughed. 'You really are *incredibly* smart, Miss Foley.' Then, taking her hand, he led her to the oak front door, which opened as if by magic without even being touched.

The interior was even swankier than the exterior, a pristine white and gold reception with a distinct trace of chlorine in the air, staffed by a severe-looking raven-haired woman who must have magicked the door open. She gave a familiar smile of greeting to Enzo before launching into a spiel of Italian that was delivered too fast for Rebecca to even attempt making sense of. Enzo conversed back at equal speed and then the next thing she knew, he was guiding her to an elevator.

'We're going to the apartment?' she asked, stepping inside it.

He pushed the button. 'My mother still owns it. I would have shown you inside my father's but he rented it and I didn't think the current tenants would be happy being woken on a Sunday morning by a stranger asking to show his…' He cut himself off mid-sentence as the doors closed, his features morphing into something she couldn't decipher before he shook his head and laughed harshly. 'Do you know, I don't have any idea how I am supposed to refer to you now.'

Rebecca's gaze fell to her bare wedding ring finger and, suddenly frightened at how much she missed the weight of her engagement ring on it and alarmed that she was letting Enzo hold her hand, unthreaded her fingers from his and hugged her arms around herself.

'It doesn't matter how you refer to me,' she said in a lighter tone than she could have hoped to manage. 'I'll be gone in four hours. I won't know.' Mercifully, she didn't have to see his expression at this statement for the elevator doors slid back open and she stepped into a small room that contained two doors.

Enzo pressed his thumb to the box beside the door on the left. The light on the box turned green and he opened the door.

Suddenly nervous, her feet refused to move across the threshold. 'She's not in, is she?'

'We wouldn't be here if she was,' he answered shortly.

'You've been in contact with her?' He must

have been if he knew his mother's current whereabouts.

'Only to tell her to stay the hell out of my life.'

'Not planning to forgive her anytime soon?'

'I will never forgive her.'

'Never is a long time.'

His clear brown eyes suddenly swooped on hers. 'Can you ever forgive *me*?'

Her heart burst into a frantic canter. 'That's different.'

'Is it? Do you think I am kidding myself that these aren't the last hours I'll ever get to spend with you? My relationship with my mother is as beyond repair as my relationship with you is. I don't expect your forgiveness, *cara*. All I hope for is that you leave Florence knowing in your heart that what I did to you was never about you, and that it is something I will regret to my dying day. But I cannot forgive her. My mother betrayed me for vengeance and betrayed me in the worst possible way.'

She swallowed. 'Because she knew you'd be publicly humiliated?'

A contortion of emotions showed in his tightened features before he flashed a smile that didn't meet his eyes. 'Come, Miss Foley, let me give you the tour.'

It was the first time since she'd demanded honesty from him that he'd evaded answering a question. Some instinct warned her not to probe.

Taking a subtle deep breath, Rebecca followed him into the apartment then found herself blinking in reaction to the sudden brightness surrounding her.

'Has it changed much since you lived here?' she asked.

'Not much.' His voice had regained the lightness from earlier but she detected an edge behind it. 'The colour scheme is the same as it has always been.'

Colour scheme? Is that what he called it?

Silvana's apartment was essentially a condensed version of her villa. Everything was white, from the soft furnishings to the marble flooring to the frames of the few paintings hanging on the white walls. Even the paintings themselves were daubed in muted hues. The only real colour came from the sun filtering through the window. Enzo's villa had the same pristine quality to it but it also had an abundance of colour and warmth. Once Rebecca had got over her shock at its palatial size and quality, she'd felt comfortable enough in it to snuggle on any of the myriad of sofas with her feet tucked under her bottom.

She didn't imagine anyone would ever feel at ease enough to sit in this sterile place: she imagined visitors just hovered. She could not begin to imagine how a small boy used to running and playing coped with being plunged into a sterility a hospital would be proud of, and as images came to mind of Enzo as that small boy, she quickly shoved them away.

She didn't want to think about his childhood. She didn't want another heartfelt conversation. Too many of his revelations had hurt her heart and all it served was to make her vulnerable when she needed to be strong in the face of what was shortly coming for her.

All she wanted now was to recapture the fizz and energy that had been alive in her veins and the light-hearted mood they'd shared since Enzo joined her on the roof terrace and, for these last few hours together, to forget the past, forget the future and live for a present she would never have again.

Grabbing his hand, she tugged at it and

smiled brightly. 'Come on, you, give me the grand tour you promised me.'

It took a moment for his dimples to appear. 'Miss Foley, your wish is my command.'

She would not think about how he'd picked up on her need for lightness without her having to say anything. Or think that maybe he needed the lightness too.

With Enzo now playing the role of tour guide, Rebecca was led into a pure white kitchen that had to be a nightmarish magnet for sticky fingers, a dining room that no one in their right mind would dare drop so much as a crumb in and then the tidiest office in the entire world. So this was where Silvana had masterminded her criminal empire...

At the other end of the apartment were the bedrooms.

'The guest room,' Enzo announced, opening the first door to which Rebecca's only thought was, *God help any guest who suffered a nosebleed in the night*... before he opened the next door. 'Robina Hood's room.'

She snickered before poking her head into a much larger room dominated by a white bed carved in the shape of swan, and then Enzo opened the last door with a flourish and Rebecca found her eyes adjusting to a space so dark he switched the light on so they could see properly.

The walls were painted a deep grey, the bedding on the king-sized bed a deep blue that matched the carpets and curtains, the wardrobes, desk and dresser black. She didn't have to ask to know he'd chosen the colour scheme and that part of it had been with annoying his mother in mind. Well-thumbed books, mostly biographies of sports stars, lined the shelves and on the wall to the left of the bed hung a faded poster of a scantily clad, pouting supermodel.

She turned to him and fixed him with her best unimpressed face.

He stalked over to her with an unapologetic shrug. 'I put that up when I was seventeen.'

'That's the kind of woman you go for?' She turned her back to him and looked again at the long-legged glossy beauty with eyes that purred seduction and experienced a sudden urge to tear it from the wall and rip it into tiny pieces.

'It was when I was a Vespa boy.'

How pathetic that she could feel jealousy towards an airbrushed woman on a teenage boy's poster. 'You must have been thrilled when you made it to the big time and could date those women.'

He slid his arms around her waist and pressed himself against her back. 'It was *very* thrilling, Miss Foley,' he murmured, resting his chin on the top of her head. 'Beautiful women like the ones I once fantasised about threw themselves at me. For a long time I thought I'd died and gone to heaven.'

'I'll bet.' She had no control over the tartness in her voice, but thrills of her own were zinging through her veins and she leaned back into his strength and closed her eyes to the poster her fingers still itched to destroy.

One of Enzo's hands splayed over her stomach and up her ribs to cup a breast that was much smaller than even the skinny supermodel's, the other flattening against her belly, holding her securely as he ground himself against her. His erection jammed hard into the small of her back. She raised herself onto her toes and pushed back against it with a moan that deepened when he squeezed her breast with just the right amount of pressure to send the zing she'd been trying so hard to find back into her veins, but deeper, needier...

'Yes, Miss Foley, I thought I'd found

heaven.' He dipped his head and nipped at her ear. 'But when the thrill wears off and you find yourself sharing your breakfast with a beautiful woman you feel nothing for and who you know feels nothing for you, you quickly learn heaven is nothing but an illusion.'

The sensation of Enzo's lips and breath against her sensitive skin was so electrifying that when he twisted her so they no longer faced the poster but a full-length mirror, she hardly noticed until she opened her eyes and saw their reflection.

His chin resting again on the top of her head, he met her stare in the mirror's reflection and undid the top two buttons of her dress. 'I had no wish to peer inside their heads,' he whispered, undoing the next button and slipping his hand through the material's opening, then sliding it under the lace of her bra to cover her naked breast.

Hot, liquid desire shot through her, melting her core and turning her legs to jelly.

Mouth now hot in her hair, eyes still locked on hers, fingers still unbuttoning her in more ways than one, his voice thickened. 'They never distracted me from my work.' He gently pinched her puckered nipple and ground himself tighter against her. 'I never watched the time crawl to when I would next see them.'

Her dress entirely undone, he dragged his mouth against her cheek and dipped his fingers beneath the lace of her knickers. 'I never felt so mad with desire that I feared the touch of their bare skin would make me lose my mind.'

He slid a finger over her swollen nub, making her jolt at the depth of the pleasure, and she slammed her hand over his to keep it there and held on tightly to stop her jellied legs from collapsing.

And then she caught the dark gleam reflecting in his hungry eyes, the intensity of it making her thundering heart skip a beat... but there was barely time to acknowledge it for Enzo turned her around and then his hot, greedy mouth was plundering hers.

Rebecca's last real thought before she dissolved into sensation was that time was running out and that this would be the last time she would ever be in his arms. The last time she would ever feel like this...

In moments, her dress and underwear were puddles on the floor, Enzo's clothes thrown with them, and they were in a naked tangle of limbs on the bed, devouring and writhing together like two starving people finding a meal in each other.

She would never know how kisses could be hard and furious and yet tender all at the same time, or how fingers could bite into flesh causing both pleasure and pain.

But that's what loving Enzo was, pleasure and pain, and the desperation thrumming so tightly with the hunger in her veins was the knowledge that soon the pleasure would be nothing but a memory. Enzo would be nothing but a memory. All this would be gone...

Holding his skull tightly, she kissed him even harder, as if the duelling of their tongues could stop the thoughts in her head, and when he wrenched his mouth away and moved down her body to pleasure her with his tongue, she screwed her eyes shut and did everything she could to banish her own consciousness.

Sensations were saturating her but no matter how hard she tried to close her mind and simply revel in the headiness of it all, the switch in her brain wouldn't turn off.

Reaching down to clasp the sides of his head, she tried to close her thighs to him. 'I need you inside of me,' she whispered urgently. Needed him inside her. Part of her.

He muttered something, Italian words she couldn't decipher, and then crawled back up her and kissed her hard enough to bruise her lips. She locked her arms around his neck and wrapped her thighs around him.

With a ragged groan, he drove deep inside her.

She cried out loudly at the glorious sensation and raised her bottom to deepen the penetration.

Scraping her fingers through his hair, their mouths fused back together…every part of them was fused…and Enzo was pounding into her, hard, frenzied, an urgent maniacal possession capturing them both, teeth and nails biting into flesh, pleasure and pain, pleasure and pain…

As desperately as Rebecca wished that she could make this last time last for ever, she could more easily hold back the tide than control the climax building inside of her, and then she was crying out again, clinging to him as waves of pleasure exploded, carrying her on an undulating crest she tried frantically to ride for as long as was humanly possible.

As if he'd been waiting for her release, Enzo's eyes opened and bore into hers, the flame from them touching her as deeply as the pleasure engulfing her before he gave a strangled groan and shudders vibrated through the whole of his body and he collapsed with his cheek tight against hers and the weight of his body covering her.

The crest she'd been riding rippled to the shore.

Neither of them moved so much as a muscle. Not for the longest time. Neither of them spoke. The only sound in the room was the matching unsteadiness of their breaths and the thrum of Rebecca's heartbeat pounding in her head. And a clock. Somewhere in this room, a clock was marking the passing seconds.

She could feel the staccato beat of Enzo's heart, she realised dimly. It was pressed against her own. Feel the last twitches of his orgasm inside her matching the last, dying spasms of her own. The dampness of his skin matched hers too.

Tears burned the back of her retinas. All she could hear now was the ticking clock, and as it grew louder in her ears, she thought how easy it would be to stay and have this completeness for the rest of her life.

But it wouldn't be for the rest of her life,

would it? She would spend the time they had together always knowing the truth, always waiting for him to casually bring up the issue of the shares, always waiting for the day he'd had his fill of her and no longer cared what went on in her head.

Oh, God, did that mean she believed he actually cared what went on in her head now?

Was she losing her *mind*? How could she possibly find anything like happiness, never mind completeness, with a man she could never trust? And this completeness...it was just sex! Perfect, beautiful, loving, desperate sex.

She was losing her mind. She had to be.

Somehow the ticking of the clock grew even louder.

How much longer did they have now? Three hours? Two?

Unable to bear her tortured thoughts any longer, she swallowed a sob and groped for something to say to break this awful, stretching silence, words that wouldn't betray the tumult of emotions battering her. 'Is there a reason Robina kept your room like a time capsule?'

The silence stretched even longer before he finally answered. 'Not that I know of.'

Shifting his weight off her, not by much, just enough so she could breathe more easily, he threaded his fingers through hers and brought her hand to his mouth, rubbing his lips over her knuckles.

Another sob tried to break free and she fought as hard as she'd ever fought in her life to keep it contained.

'Did she think you would move back in?' She remembered Enzo telling her he'd moved into the apartment above his first jewellery store the moment the lease for it became available when he was nineteen.

His nose nuzzled into her cheek. 'I have long given up trying to guess what goes through my mother's head.'

'Maybe she kept it like this in case you ever changed your mind.'

'Unlikely.'

'As a reminder then, of the son you'd been before you moved out and became a man.'

He lifted his head. Gaze tight on hers, his brow furrowed. 'Why are you trying to humanise her?'

'Because she's your mother and her being a vindictive Robina Hood doesn't change that.' A short burst of laughter at what she was saying flew from her lips. What did it matter to her if Enzo cut his mother from his life completely? They were as bad as each other, something she needed to reinforce in her mind with concrete. And her heart.

A whole day had now passed since she'd received Silvana's package and despite Rebecca's best efforts, Enzo had managed to re-humanise himself fully in her eyes. Now, with the desperation of their lovemaking still alive in her veins, she was in the most dreadful danger; in danger of forgiving what he'd done to her and forgetting what he was capable of.

'What pushed you over the edge and made you threaten her?' she asked, trying her hardest to fight the panic now clawing back at her. 'It's not a very Italian thing to do is it, ratting out your own flesh and blood.'

He gave a grunt-like laugh and finally withdrew from her. 'If she'd forced my hand, I would have had to hand my citizenship in.'

Terrified at how bereft she felt with that last connection between them gone, Rebecca scrambled to sit up. 'Exactly.' She grabbed a pillow and placed it to her chest before drawing her knees up and wrapping her arms around her legs. 'And you waited until you were twenty-eight, so something must have spurred you on.'

The eyes that had narrowed while watching her cover her nudity held her stare for what felt like an age before he sat up too. 'Because I couldn't live with the fear any more.'

Wishing he'd said his reasons had been because of a threat to his business, Rebecca pressed her thighs to the pillow against her chest even more firmly and tightened her arms' hold around them, knowing even as she did it that this was a variation of what she'd done in the aftermath of their first lovemaking, a futile attempt at using her body to protect her heart, which would only make sense if her heart could still be protected from him.

But it couldn't, and she understood exactly what he meant about living with the fear because it was the same reason she still needed to walk away from him, otherwise she would be doomed to living with that fear too, for as long as it took for Enzo to walk away from *her*.

'How much longer could her luck have held?' he asked tautly. 'If she wouldn't quit, not even for my sake, then I had no choice but to force her—her reputation is as important to her as mine is to me. A police investigation into her business, even a fruitless one, would have destroyed that reputation and she knew it. I wish I could say I did it for noble reasons and that I believed even the scummy people she targeted didn't deserve to have their jewellery collections stolen from them but that would be a lie, and I have promised not to lie to you. I made my threat because it would have killed me to see my mother thrown into a prison cell.'

Rebecca pictured Silvana; tall, beautiful, whip-smart, brimming with energy. Locking her into a prison cell would be like locking a Bengali tiger into a tiny cage.

Despite herself, she pictured a young Enzo too, grieving the loss of his father and the loss of everything that was familiar, slowly growing up with the fear gripping his chest increasing as his mother's criminality and the implications of what would happen if she were caught became clearer to him.

He wasn't that child any more. She had to remember that. Had to. *Had* to.

# CHAPTER ELEVEN

'Is it a coincidence that you made your threat when you were the same age as your father when he died?' The question formed before Rebecca's brain had even thought of it.

Enzo's eyes narrowed. A groove lined his forehead. The corners of his lips twitched before he finally answered. 'And you believe you don't know me?' He shook his head and gave a disbelieving laugh. 'It was no coincidence. Turning twenty-eight was a big deal for me. As a child, it seemed *old* but the closer I got to it…' Grimacing, he dragged his fingers through his dark hair, mussing it up even more than it already was from their lovemaking. 'I spent much of the year doing all the reckless, dangerous things a single man with too much money can do.'

Ice prickled her spine and chest, goose bumps rising on her arms. If she weren't holding her legs so tightly she would rub them for warmth. 'What kinds of things?'

'I climbed Everest. Went white-water rafting down Nepal's Karnali River. Completed six skydives. Jumped off the Kawarau Bridge. Pickled my liver too many times to be considered clever or advisable.' His eyes closed before locking back on to hers. 'I had this feeling inside me that if this was to be my last year on this earth then I needed to live it and experience every shot of adrenaline it had to offer, and while I was on this voyage of destructive discovery, I came to the conclusion that I could not meet my maker without knowing my mother was safe from her own destructive genes. If I was to survive to see twenty-nine I could no longer live in fear of her liberty being taken from her.' Another twitch of his lips. 'Even if she did deserve it.'

*Even if she did deserve it…*

A paraphrasing of the same words Rebecca had told herself earlier on the terrace when she'd realised she would never be able to use the Claflin Diamond shares as a weapon against him.

'So you gave her the ultimatum,' she said slowly. A pulse was beating loudly in her head, nausea roiling in her stomach.

'I did. And she never forgave me. I expected that. I expected she would seek her vengeance. I crossed a line.' His eyes flashed. 'What I did not expect was that in her vengeance she would not only cross the line but firebomb it.'

'Sure about that are you?' She lifted her chin to look him square in the eye. 'Because from what you've told me about her, you should have expected it.'

Enzo's shock at the change in her tone was apparent in the way his head reared back before he stilled and his pupils darkened with anger. 'My mother's reputation is everything to her. My humiliation is her humiliation.'

'I'm not disputing that—she must have factored that in when she decided to drop her firebomb and decided it was a price worth paying, but even so, it's a bit neat and easy for you to point the finger of blame at Robina rather than take responsibility for your own actions.'

His stare had become like granite. 'I do take responsibility. Full responsibility. I have done from the start.'

'Then accept that *you* sabotaged our wedding.' Laughter that tinged on the hysterical burst out of her. She couldn't help it, had no control over it. '*You* sabotaged our wedding and put your business in danger, Enzo, not Robina. You told your mother when you knew she was biding her time to take her revenge. Maybe you *do* have a conscience. Maybe that's what drove you into telling her—deep down you wanted her to do your dirty work for you and save you the bother of having to make the confession yourself.'

As the taunts continued flying out of her mouth. Rebecca realised she was trying to provoke a fight. She wanted him to defend himself and shout at her, to call her cruel, disparaging names, give her something to latch onto to hate him for and stop the awful, desperate longing inside her to stay.

'To be honest, I don't really care,' she continued. 'I don't care why you confessed to her or her reasons in exposing you to me, I'm just grateful that she *did* expose you as the liar you are and stopped me from making the biggest mistake of my life. The two of you are as bad as each other. Seriously, Enzo, don't cut her off. You deserve one another.'

So intent had Rebecca been on saving herself from herself that she barely registered Enzo's eyes had become devoid of all life and his features a blank canvas devoid of emotion, not until she found herself enveloped in the loudest silence of her life with the air between them so taut that she felt the slightest pinch would see it snap.

The silence stretched.

She tried to draw in a breath but her airways had closed.

Then his nostrils flared.

With a short bow of his head, he climbed off the bed in one fluid movement and reached for his shorts.

'Get dressed,' he said curtly. 'We're going back to the villa.'

The ride back to the villa was as different from the ride into the city as night was to day. Where earlier they'd ridden with a fizzing air of joy, the mood now had a distinctly different, darker hue. Enzo hadn't spoken a single word since telling Rebecca to get dressed.

She'd dressed in the bathroom. She'd put her clothes back on calmly but when she'd tidied her hair in front of the mirror, there had been a tremor in her hands.

When she'd returned to the bedroom, Enzo had gone. She'd found him in the sterile kitchen looking out of the window, drinking a glass of water. His shoulder muscles had bunched before he'd turned to face her. She'd raised her chin, holding her breath at what she'd find in his eyes but finding…nothing. Suddenly frightened at what he was hiding behind his shuttered stare, she'd quickly ripped her gaze from him and looked out of the kitchen window. That's when she'd seen what he'd been staring out at. She couldn't believe she hadn't noticed it earlier.

The kitchen window overlooked the cathedral where Rebecca had left him standing at the altar. The cathedral she'd humiliated him to the whole world in. And now, as he took the road that led to his villa, the press pack emerged in the distance just before Enzo turned onto the narrow dust track, and a stab of guilt cut through her.

*He'd* brought this on himself, she reminded herself. Enzo. Not her. She had nothing to feel guilty about. She'd been nothing but a pawn, not only in the game between him and her grandfather but between Enzo and his mother.

But she wished now that the pain of her emotions hadn't got the better of her and she'd chosen a less public way of calling the wedding off.

She hadn't done it to punish him. Truth

was, she'd been in no fit state to think at all. If she had been then she would have…

What? Given him a chance to explain?

Explain *what*? His side? There was no side, only the truth, and her grandfather's will had revealed the truth. Enzo had never loved her. He was the worst of all liars. He'd used her for his own ends.

*You could have given him a chance.*

She closed her eyes. This was all pointless. She couldn't change the past any more than Enzo could.

Knowing this didn't stop her hand from flying to her throat when Enzo brought the Vespa to a stop beside the garage's rear entrance and she looked at her watch.

Eleven fifty.

Her vision swam. Where had the time gone?

Closing her eyes to clear them, she took a deep breath and unstrapped the helmet.

Enzo made no move to take it off her. He simply stood with his hands rammed in his pockets, his jaw set, gaze fixed in the distance. His hair was sticking up in all directions.

Apologies for the home truths she'd flung at him formed on her tongue. Somehow, she bit back them back. She'd only spoken the truth. This stoniness, though, was coming close to unbearable.

Blurring him from her eyes, she pulled the helmet off then climbed off the Vespa. This was what she wanted after all. Distance between them. The ability to walk away on legs that didn't stumble beneath her.

The pulsing in her head and roiling nausea in her stomach flared up again as she followed him inside the villa.

'I'm going to get my things together,' she said quietly when they'd crossed the reception room.

He jerked a nod and uttered his first words since telling her to get dressed. 'I will get Frank to bring your cases down.'

'No need. They're not heavy.' Hating his remoteness, and hating that she hated it, she tried to inject some humour. 'Well, they *are* heavy, but I've lugged them up and down the stairs so many times recently that I'm in danger of developing muscles.'

His dimples didn't even pretend to appear at this. 'Where will you go?'

'Home.'

His jaw clenched. 'England?'

'It's my home.'

His eyes closed, face almost seeming to suck in on itself before he bowed his head and stepped away from her. 'I will get the paperwork for the shares ready for you.'

'The transfer's already been done?' There was still an hour until the deadline she'd imposed. In the back of her mind she'd imagined him dragging it all out until the last possible minute.

He turned back to look at her. 'I received the notification of completion when we were eating our breakfast.'

'This morning?'

There was no apology in his stare. 'Consider my failure to tell you another mark against my name.'

If Rebecca put all her stuff by the front door one more time she thought an indent might just appear in the terracotta flooring. Through the window at the side of the door she saw the large black car had reappeared, parked in the same spot as yesterday, ready to whisk her away.

As she padded barefoot across the reception room she blinked away the image of shattered marble that flashed in her eyes and then, as she entered the main living area and found Enzo at the bar pouring himself a Scotch, a wave of déjà vu hit her.

Full circle.

'Gin and tonic?' he asked, keeping his back to her.

'No thank you. I'll just take the shares and get going.' No more excuses. They'd dragged it out—*she'd* dragged it out—long enough.

If he hadn't had her passport in his safe, she could have followed her instincts and fled immediately to England from the cathedral.

But if she'd done that, she would never have experienced the heaven of making love with Enzo.

Whether she would live to regret that joy, only time would tell. Right now, she didn't want to think about it. She just wanted to go while she still had control of herself, without making a scene.

He turned, and held up a gin glass practically filled to the brim. 'I've already made it. You might as well drink it. The shares and business documents are on the sideboard. There are things about them I need to discuss with you.'

She spotted the envelope they were contained in. 'We've had plenty of time to discuss them.' She didn't add that he could have told her over breakfast that the deed had been done and that they were hers and discussed whatever he thought needed talking about then.

'It wasn't the right time before.'

Not responding, she pulled the documents out of the envelope and gave them a quick scan. He'd stuck by his word and transferred them. For that alone, she would give him some credit.

'You are welcome to get a lawyer to check it all over for you but I assure you, everything is in order. They have already been digitally transferred into your name. You are officially my business partner.'

That took her aback. She'd never considered it like that. Not in those terms.

As if reading her mind, he gave a wry smile and raised his full tumbler of Scotch. First taking a large drink of it, he then placed her gin on the glass table next to the squishy sofa she favoured and sat himself stiffly on an armchair she'd never seen him use before. 'I did consider transferring the whole of Claflin Diamonds to you but it would have been meaningless. You would just have seen it as another performance.'

Yes, she thought. She would have seen it like that.

He nodded at her drink. 'Please. Sit. Drink. What I have to tell you should not take long. I have booked a flight for you to England that leaves in three hours. The ticket's been sent to your email. You will still leave here by one and have plenty of time to reach the airport in good time for it.'

'Oh. Well…thank you.' Knowing it would be churlish to refuse after he'd gone out of his way to book her onto a flight, something she hadn't thought of doing for herself, Rebecca perched on the sofa with both feet firmly on the floor, and had a quick sip of her perfectly made gin.

Why hadn't she thought to book herself onto a flight? The notion hadn't crossed her mind, not even when she'd considered fleeing in the middle of the night.

'Are you hungry?' he asked.

'No.' The cramped feeling in her stomach had returned.

'Neither am I.' He took another, even bigger drink of his Scotch then cradled the tumbler in both hands and gazed moodily into the amber liquid.

'The shares, Enzo?'

His lips tightened and his shoulders rose. A swirl of emotions played over his face before his features rearranged themselves into something unreadable and he met her stare. 'Do you remember me telling you that your grandfather turned down a much better offer for the business so he could partner with me?'

'Is this relevant?'

'Yes. Are you not curious as to why he chose the riskier option of partnering with a young man whose only jewellery store was making a loss? Our deal paid his debts off but if we'd failed, he would have been left with nothing.'

She pinched the bridge of her nose. 'Honestly? I don't care. Probably he admired your burning ambition, but you didn't fail so why does this matter?'

'I had not proved myself in any way for that ambition to be anything other than a dream. I've come to believe the reason your grandfather took that risk was because he thought he saw in me a way to make amends to his conscience for what he did to your mother.'

Rebecca shot to her feet so abruptly she knocked the table and sent gin and tonic sloshing over the rim of her glass. 'You said you wanted to discuss the shares and the business, not give me a history lesson.'

'It is one and the same thing.'

'Then I don't want to hear it.' She stomped to the box of tissues on the side and grabbed a handful of them.

'I know you don't but as you intend to walk out of my life for good at any minute, I ask that you do me the courtesy of listening to what I have to say.'

Lifting the glass, she flattened the tissues over the spilt liquid. 'I don't want to hear justifications for his behaviour.'

'There is no justification for that. He should never have forced your mother into making that choice and should never have cut her off because of it. It was his inability to admit to his mistakes that stopped him making amends to her.'

Abandoning her efforts to clean the spill, Rebecca angrily wiped her hand on the side of her dress and walked quickly to the door. 'Forget it. I don't want to hear *any* of this.'

'I know you don't, but you have to.'

'No.'

Before she could reach the door, Enzo had passed her to block the exit.

Folding his arms over his chest, he stared emotionlessly down at her.

Rather than argue, she turned to leave by the wide French door that opened onto the garden.

'It is locked. If you want the key, it's in my back pocket. The dining room door is also locked.'

She spun back round.

He was still blocking the door, body and expression immovable.

Another wave of déjà vu. Another full circle reached.

'You will hear what I have to say, Rebecca,' he said quietly but with an implacability that sent shivers lacing her spine.

'Don't *call* me that,' she whispered, taking a step back.

'Rebecca. Rebecca Emily Foley. A beautiful name for a beautiful woman. Rebecca, I have respected your wishes as to what I can and cannot say and how I refer to you—'

'That wasn't respecting my wishes, it was

because you knew I'd destroy the business if you didn't.'

Eyes flashing dangerously, his voice rose for the first time. 'When will you understand that I no longer care about the business? I agreed to your terms because I hoped the time I managed to negotiate with you would be enough for you to realise the truth for yourself, but you won't open your eyes to see and now I have nothing left to lose. Destroy Claflin Diamonds if you want. Destroy my entire business. I don't care. Go outside and tell the waiting press and the world what I did to you. I don't care. The minute you walk out of here my life as it is is over, but I will not let you walk away without hearing the full truth, so if you want to be gone by one o'clock I suggest you sit down, open your ears and let me speak.'

White noise swam through Rebecca's head. Her heart was thumping madly, the beats adding to the cacophony in her brain, making it hard to think coherently.

She had three choices. One: fight her way past him. Two: launch herself through the patio doors. Three: sit down and let him have his say. Only the second option held any appeal. It was by far the least painful of the options with the only wounds likely to be her body being torn to shreds from the glass she'd jump through. To fight her way past Enzo meant having to touch him. Smell him. All the things that played havoc with her senses and confuddled her brain. To sit down and listen meant…

Nothing, she realised. He couldn't *make* her listen. If she concentrated hard enough, she could block his words out.

Storming back to her seat, she drank the entirety of what hadn't spilt of her gin and plonked herself down, crossing her legs and folding her arms tightly. 'Go on then. Get it over with.'

His chest rose slowly before he gave a sharp nod and retook his own seat. His gaze locked on her. Let him look, she thought. Enzo staring into her eyes didn't mean her ears would listen.

'Your grandfather was a self-made man. He started with nothing. He despised your father, not because of the age he left school or the job he did but for his lack of ambition. Your grandfather equated ambition with success. He saw in me a kindred spirit, a young man he could help mould in the way your mother refused to be moulded. I am certain that is part of the reason why he went so far as to cut your mother off—she refused to be your grandfather's carbon copy in female form.'

Currently trying to picture herself standing on a beach somewhere hot and imagining the feel of warm salt water lapping at her feet, Rebecca suddenly realised she was thinking of her idealised version of Mauritius and quickly tried to imagine herself somewhere else.

Mauritius was where they were supposed to fly that evening for their honeymoon.

'He always expected her to come crawling back. He never dreamed she would be taken so young.' He grimaced. 'People don't. We expect those we love to become like Methuselah before they die. We do not expect to lose our children. Her early death set his demons off. He never stopped loving her. And he always loved you.'

She snorted quietly. Disparagingly.

'He did love you, Rebecca.'

'He didn't know me.'

'He kept your graduation photo on his desk.'

Her head jerked at this and, against her

will, her eyes focused on his. 'How on earth did he get that?'

He shrugged. 'He had his ways and means. He kept tabs on your mother over the years. Your graduation photo replaced an older one from when you were a little girl blowing out the candles of your birthday cake. I can't remember how old you were in it. Ten, maybe. Your graduation made him proud. Not having a relationship with you was his greatest dying regret and why I think he did what he did with his will.'

Her snort at this was much louder. 'He screwed you over because he regretted not having a relationship with me? Yep, that makes a whole heap of sense.'

'By the time he died, your grandfather loved two people. You and me. He loved you because you were his flesh and blood. He loved me because what started as a business relationship where he was the master and I the apprentice became a mutually respectful friendship. There was a great deal of affection between us. Even when Beresi took off and my wealth mushroomed and I no longer needed him as my mentor, our friendship endured. I have become certain that writing that clause in his will was his way of forcing you and me together.'

# CHAPTER TWELVE

THE DOLPHIN POD Rebecca had been trying to envisage herself swimming with evaporated into a mist. She stared incredulously at Enzo. 'Did you drink the whole bottle of Scotch while I was getting my stuff together?'

He held the now half-full glass aloft. 'I should have. It would make all this easier to deal with.'

'I'm not stopping you.'

'I will wait until you leave before I do that. For now, it is good to be clear-headed, and I do not want you thinking this is all coming from the mouth of a drunk.' He laughed grimly. 'I am certain now that it is what your grandfather wanted to happen. You and me. He would often show me your photo and say what a beautiful young woman you'd turned into and that it would be a lucky man who married you. I used to think he was just being a proud grandfather but now...' He swallowed some more of his Scotch. 'You and I were the only two people he loved and the two people with him when he died.'

Rebecca, having had to quit trying to imagine herself somewhere else, felt her heart somersault into her stomach.

'After his diagnosis, your photo was moved from his desk to his bedside table. Always he would look at it.' Then he added matter-of-factly, 'After his death, I learned to hate your face.'

She recoiled, inwardly and outwardly.

His eyes rang with self-loathing. 'Yes, Rebecca, I admit I hated you. I was the closest thing Ray had to family. His wife and daughter were dead and his granddaughter wanted nothing to do with him. It was me he named his next of kin with the hospital. It was me who arranged for him to have twenty-four-hour care in his home and who moved into his guest room so I could make sure they didn't cut corners with his care. I did all that because I loved him like he was my blood and then I read his will and learned that he had, as you put it, stitched me up like a kipper, and betrayed me for the granddaughter who'd rejected him and who he'd only seen in photographs.' That awful grim smile curled on his face. 'He set things up so we would be forced to meet. Whether he predicted my reaction to the clause I cannot say. I discounted the other routes I could have taken to overturn his will or come to an agreement with you because in my fury with him, my heart was filled with vengeance… I am afraid that is my inherited blood from my mother coming out in me…and the target for my vengeance was you, Rebecca Emily Foley.

'I had people watch your every move. I kept close to you. I was waiting for a plausible opportunity to hook you in. I knew it would be easy to seduce you because my money and the looks I have been blessed with mean women are easy for me. There is not a woman alive who I have wanted who has not wanted me in return.' He spoke as if revealing a not particularly important fact. 'And then my opportunity came along and finally I came face to face with my nemesis.'

He broke away to take another drink, closing his eyes as he drained the last of his Scotch.

'I built you up in my head as a Medusa figure but meeting you in the flesh…' He took another long breath through his nose. 'You were so *nice*.' He laughed disbelievingly. 'Believe me, I was not used to nice. I was used to calculators. But you were nice and witty, and your *smile*... *Dio*, your smile. But I was set on my path and I was still too full of anger and hurt to see that I should step off it but every day my conscience was getting louder. I remember the first time we kissed—*Dio*, I can still feel it—and you would not believe how it made me feel. I could not believe it myself. It felt like you'd drugged me, and then the night you told me you were a virgin...' He stretched his hand over his forehead and rubbed it. 'I think I was already in love with you then.'

'No!' The word had shot out of Rebecca's mouth before she was even aware of the terror grabbing hold of her or aware that she'd jumped back to her feet.

'Yes.' Enzo's stare was bleak but unwavering. 'You need to hear this as much as I need to say it. No more hiding, Rebecca. It is too late for that. I told you last night, your virginity changed everything for me. My conscience would not let me take you to bed, but still there was a war going on in my head and if I had realised what was happening to me instead of continually justifying my actions to myself, I would have confessed everything to you. I wish to hell I had confessed it all then.'

'Not as much as I wish you had,' she whispered, holding her stomach tightly.

'*Cara*, I will *never* forgive myself for what I did to you. I let my hurt and fury drive me to vengeance against a woman who had done *nothing* to deserve it apart from exist. I was fully prepared to detest you, but meeting you and hating you was impossible. You brought something out in me that I didn't understand, and I didn't understand it because I'd never felt it before. I had never walked a pavement with anyone before you and needed to walk along the kerb so I would be the one that was hit if a car swerved off the road, and I wish like hell that I'd understood what the hell was happening to me before I proposed to you.' He gripped his hair, the knuckles of his fingers white. 'You made me wait so long for your answer that I thought my heart had stopped beating and then when you finally said yes… I have never had a rush of blood to my head like it. That was the moment that it hit me that I loved you and I have been living in dread of losing you ever since.'

Rebecca's legs finally gave way beneath

her and she sank back onto the sofa. 'Why are you doing this to me? Haven't you hurt me enough?'

'If I could take back all the pain that I've caused you and inject it into my bloodstream then I would. I wanted to tell you the truth. I knew that to marry you on a lie was unforgivable and I tried many times in the months before our wedding to find the words and throw myself on your mercy but the fear in my heart...' He punched his chest. 'I've never known fear like it; worse than the fear I had of my mother being imprisoned. It left me so damn *cold* to imagine my life without you because for the first time in so very long I'd found true happiness, but the longer I left it, the colder I felt.'

He dragged his fingers down his face. 'I have thought of what you said about me sabotaging our wedding and I think you could be right.' The ghost of a smile flickered on his face. 'Your grandfather taught me irony and I have to say it is ironic that if he were still alive, it is him I would have turned to.' He gave a bitter laugh and shrugged. 'I don't know. I wasn't thinking straight when I confessed to my mother and two bottles of red wine did not help, but the closer the wedding got the harder it was for me to live with what I was doing to you and everything you were giving up for me. I never intended to tell her anything, not consciously, and while I know I have no one to blame but myself for all this, I will never forgive her either, because she took her vengeance knowing she would destroy the one thing that mattered the most in the whole world to me—you. Your love.'

Reeling at everything he'd just confessed, aching to believe him, aching even harder to forgive him, Rebecca hauled herself back to her wobbly legs and staggered to the bar.

'You cannot imagine what it has been like for me having you in my life,' he said quietly as she groped blindly for two glasses. Blindly because her eyes were swimming. But she didn't have to be able to see to sense Enzo rising to his feet and closing some of the distance between them. 'Before you, I enjoyed my life and the advantages my wealth gave me but always there was something missing. I never understood what it was until I met you. That something was you.'

Having just poured them both a hefty slug of whatever had come out of the closest bottle to hand, Rebecca pushed one drink along the bar for Enzo and took a large mouthful of her own. Vodka. Strong enough to make her eyes water and burn her chest. Strong enough to clear her mind of the haze she'd fallen into listening to him.

'Do you know, Enzo, words are really easy to say,' she said, keeping her back to him. 'I want to believe you. I would give *anything* to believe you. But I can't.' She downed the rest of the clear liquid, slammed the glass on the marble bar and spun around to face him.

He was leaning back against the floor-to-ceiling window. His arms were folded, his chest rising and falling in rapid, ragged motions.

'I'm sorry but you're not a teenager,' she told him quietly. 'You're a thirty-three-year-old man, worth billions, and all from your own hard work. It is beyond credulity for me to believe you were too frightened of losing me to tell me the truth if guilt has been eating you for months in the way you claim.'

His eyes bore into hers; lasers trying to drill into her mind before he unpeeled himself from the window and took the five steps to the bar. He closed his fingers around the vodka she'd poured him. 'What day is it?' he asked.

Taken off guard at the question, she had to grope for it. 'Sunday?'

'*Sì*. Sunday.' He raised the glass and peered into it in the same way he'd studied his Scotch. 'A day when business is closed.' He turned sharply to her. 'Have you not questioned how I was able to transfer the shares into your name and add your name to the business in such a short time frame and over a weekend?'

'Because you're Enzo Beresi and always get your own way about everything.'

His lips curled. 'I do not walk on water. They were completed so quickly because I had already set everything in motion. My plan was to give you all the documents the morning after our wedding over breakfast and confess everything because my one hope was that us being married meant you would feel obliged to try and forgive me.' He raised his face to the ceiling and muttered something under his breath before looking back at her. 'But you wouldn't have forgiven me, would you?'

Blinking rapidly to fight the burn of tears stabbing again at her eyes, she swallowed. 'I guess we'll never know.'

He shook his head slowly and brought the

vodka to his lips before changing his mind and lowering it back to the bar. 'No. You wouldn't have forgiven me. I understand that now. And I understand now why I could never bring myself to tell you.' He brought the vodka back to his mouth but still didn't drink. 'I never realised why the thought of telling you made my chest cold when you are the best person I have ever known. You have a warmth to you, Rebecca, and believe me, in my world that is rare. *Dio*, you won Robina over in ten minutes—that is normally the time it takes her to decide that she hates someone. I saw all the goodbye cards you got from your school. The children and their parents, your colleagues…they all loved you. A woman like you…' He rubbed the glass over his chin. 'But now I understand it. It became clear to me last night. I kept the truth from you because I knew in my heart that you were waiting for a reason to end things with me. Discovering your grandfather's will was the excuse you were looking for. If it hadn't been that, you would have found something else.' And with that he finally downed the vodka in one huge swallow, smacking his lips together and then wiping his mouth with the back of his hand.

Utterly gobsmacked, it took a moment for Rebecca's vocal cords to work. 'Honestly, I can't believe what I'm hearing. I wasn't looking for an excuse for anything, and I can't believe you're blaming me for *your* lies. I gave up everything to be with you. I would *never* have left you.'

Weariness seemed to make him compress into himself. 'I am not blaming you for anything, *cara*. This whole situation is on me. I created it and I will have to live with the consequences for the rest of my life.' Then he straightened and looked at his watch. 'It is nearly one o'clock. You should go. My driver is waiting for you. Tell him not to run over any of the press—they will have their cameras trained on the car. He is an excellent driver and I would hate to lose him to a prison cell.' He stretched an arm, coming within millimetres of brushing against her, and wrapped his hand around the bottle of vodka.

Pulling the bottle to him, Enzo cast her another glance with eyes that had lost all animation. 'Please, Rebecca. It is time for you to leave and for me to pickle my liver. Excuse me for not seeing you out but I have never been into masochism.'

He unscrewed the lid but before he could pour the liquid into the glass, Rebecca surprised them both by snatching the bottle from him. 'You can pickle yourself in a minute, but first I want you to tell me why you thought I was looking for a reason to leave you because, honestly, that's the most ridiculous thing I've ever heard in my life. I was *nuts* about you.'

'Excellent use of past tense there,' he muttered.

'What do you expect?' she cried. 'You have destroyed my trust. I would give anything to put this behind me and put my trust back in you but I can't.'

'And I cannot blame you for that but I think the word you mean is *won't*.' Taking back hold of the bottle, he prised her fingers from it, poured himself another generous measure and brought it to his mouth. 'Seriously, Rebecca, go. I've said all I need to say. Leave me to drink.'

Impulse and rising fury had her pushing his hand before he could drink. The glass tipped, spilling vodka over his T-shirt. 'Don't tell me what I meant—I meant *can't*, now tell me where you got the idea that I was just looking for a reason to leave you.'

His jaw clenched. He ran his hand over the spilled liquid soaking into his clothes and, without saying a word, poured himself a replacement and drank it in one swallow.

When he turned his face back to her, his eyes were flashing dangerously. '*Can't* is an excuse. *Won't* is honest. You have always doubted my feelings for you.'

'For damn good reason!'

He leaned down so they were eyeball to eyeball. 'I love you. I have always loved you. I will always love you. I would walk on broken glass if it meant you would give me another chance but you won't because you're too damned scared. It is what I tried to talk to you about last night but you shut me down. You never believed in my love, not deep down, because your own insecurities make you doubt yourself too much.'

'Poppycock.'

'Is it?' A pulse throbbed in his temple. 'You felt like the third wheel in your parents' marriage.'

'Not that again. For the last time, I never meant to say that.'

'I know. But you did and that's what made sense of everything to me.' He stared at her for a long, long time before his shoulders dropped and compassion filled his velvet timbre. 'Your father had a fatal heart attack days after your mother died.'

It felt like she'd been scalded without any warning. 'What's that got to do with anything?'

'Everything. In his grief, he left you behind and left you alone.'

The burn he'd scalded her with drained out of her along with all Rebecca's blood. 'And I thought you couldn't stoop any lower than you already have...' she whispered hoarsely. 'My father was overweight. He was in agony over Mum's death. His heart couldn't take the strain.'

'I do not doubt it and I do not doubt that he loved you so do not for a second think I am saying that or implying it. Your father didn't choose his heart attack any more than my father chose to have an aneurysm but it happened. My father loved me and your parents loved you. It is your perception of your place in your family that I am talking about. You lived under the shadow of your parents' love for each other—you described it yourself as a fable and I can understand why; they were a modern day Romeo and Juliet but with a happier ending. From everything you have told me, they were as happy and loved each other as much at their deaths as when they first married, but somewhere along the way you came to believe that they loved each other more than they loved you and that it was because of this love that they left you behind.'

She backed away from him on legs that had become like jelly. 'I've thought a lot of not very nice things about you these last twenty-odd hours but I never thought you could be this cruel.'

Turning his back to her, he said, 'I made a promise never to lie to you again, but you wanted this conversation, *cara*, not me. I'd already said all I wanted to say. I just wanted to be left alone to drown myself in alcohol because every extra minute you are here cuts the wound deeper.' To make his point, he poured himself another vodka.

Rebecca took another step away from him. 'Then I shall go.'

'Good. Don't forget the package. My English lawyer's details are in it. When you decide what you want to do with the shares, contact him about it. He will act as a go-between for us. I would be grateful if you do not contact me. I think it best for both our sakes that we have a clean break.'

'I think that's best too.' How had she thought it would be cleaner this way? What had she been thinking?

After everything they'd been through, leaving like this was hell on earth.

As she picked up the package, she saw him lift his head and knew he'd tipped more vodka into his mouth. Knew, too, that Enzo would make good on his promise of pickling his liver. He'd lost.

But she'd lost too.

Her fingers closed on the door handle she could hardly see for the tears blinding her.

'Rebecca.'

His back was still turned to her but his face was turned in profile.

She swallowed a sob. 'Yes?'

His voice was so low she had to concentrate with everything she had to hear him. 'I cannot tell you if your perceptions about your parents were wrong but I know they loved you, very much. When your grandfather kept tabs on your mother he would have photos taken. I saw some of them once, not long after we went into business together. You must have been twelve or thirteen. You and your parents were on a picnic in some woods. I do not know what the occasion was but I remember feeling envy at the way your mother was captured looking at you. It was an expression my mother has never given me.'

She opened the door.

'One more thing.'

She stilled to listen to his last ever words to her.

'Your expectations of marriage were not unrealistic. Married or not, you will always be the most important person in my life.'

# CHAPTER THIRTEEN

SOMEHOW REBECCA MADE it to the front door without stumbling. Her legs were still holding her up. All her possessions except for her handbag and sandals had been taken from where she'd left them. She guessed Frank had taken them out to the waiting car.

Rubbing at her leaking eyes, she slipped the sandals on. Should have left her ankle boots. Now she'd have to root through her stuff for them before the flight so her feet didn't get cold. She hated having cold feet.

The last thing she did before leaving the villa was dig her sunglasses out of her handbag and put them on. She was glad she'd remembered to do that when she stepped outside. The sun, strong since she'd watched it come to life, was now scorching, the villa's grounds bathed in yellow from its rays.

Too intent on putting one foot in front of

the other without her legs giving up on her before she reached the car, the dozens and dozens of cameras flashing on the other side of the electric fence hardly registered, nor the loud shouts being hurled at her.

The driver got out and opened the back door.

Inside, she fastened her seat belt.

The car slowly rolled forwards. A short wait and then it drove through the electric gates. Camera lenses were pressed against the windows, flashes going off, but the tinted glass dulled the effect.

She clenched her teeth together and refused to look anywhere but forwards.

And then the cameras were gone and the car was gaining speed and Rebecca was, finally, on her way home.

Pressing her cheek against the door, she closed her eyes. A tear trickled under her sunglasses and down her chin. She wiped it away. Another fell. Soon her sunglasses were so wet that she took them off and absently placed them beside her.

The more the miles slipped by and the further she was taken from Enzo, the more acute the pulsing agony in her heart.

She saw a sign for the airport. Which airline had he booked her with? Knowing Enzo, the plushest airline. Knowing Enzo, she'd be travelling in the highest class the airline had to offer.

In five hours from now, they were supposed to be taking his private jet to Mauritius for their honeymoon. Enzo had suggested it because it was a paradise he'd never visited before. He'd wanted them to experience it for the first time together. Rebecca would have been happy to go anywhere so long as it was with him.

She pressed her knuckles to her forehead and tried as hard as she'd ever tried at anything to banish him from her thoughts.

What would happen to the suitcases she'd packed for their honeymoon the other day? Frank had taken them so they could be loaded into the car...

Were they in the boot of *this* car? Would she get to the airport and the driver unload them?

No sooner had this thought came into her head than an image of Enzo standing in the doorway of her bedroom followed, laughing at the sheer amount of clothes bulging out of the open cases.

'You don't need to pack any clothes, *cara*,'

he'd murmured seductively, stepping to her to wrap his arms around her waist. 'Our honeymoon will be spent in bed.'

Her heart racing frantically, Rebecca breathed in as deeply as she could and glimpsed another road sign for the airport.

*Why* hadn't she booked her own flight back to England? Or thought to get Frank to book it for her?

It was when she saw the third airport sign that a pain cramped in her chest, so acute that she doubled over with a howl.

Struggling to breathe, she crossed her shaking hands over her heart. Her knees were knocking together, every part of her trembling. She'd thought the pain from losing her parents had been enough to kill her, but this...

This was a different kind of grief, and it came to her in a vivid, painful flash what the difference was. Her parents had been taken from her. She was taking herself from Enzo.

Taking herself away from the man who'd blown away the cherry blossom that had landed in her hair when he'd taken her to Japan during her school's half-term break. The man who'd stroked her hair for hours when she'd been curled up next to him on the sofa suffering menstrual cramps. The man whose smile could have powered the earth when he'd watched her face during her first sunrise on his terrace. The man who'd secretly had her father's old, battered vintage car restored *for her*.

Another realisation punched her. Rebecca's mind had refused to let her think about booking a flight back to England because, at a subconscious level, a part of her brain was working in tandem with her heart. England wasn't her home any more. Enzo was.

Maybe he was too much like his mother when it came to his need for vengeance but at least he could admit to his mistakes and had tried to put them right. That had to count. And couldn't she be accused of being like the grandfather she detested for his treatment of her mother? Hadn't he refused to put right his relationship with his only child even when his actions proved how much he'd missed having her in his life? What had stopped him from reaching out to her? Pride? Sheer stubbornness? Or as Enzo had said, a refusal to admit to his mistakes? She would never know because it was all too late. The dead didn't speak.

Is that what she wanted for herself? To live

the rest of her life with regret? To reach old bones haunted by demons of the past?

Rebecca was barely aware of undoing her seat belt and flinging herself forward to bang on the dividing window. 'Take me back!' she cried, then remembered the intercom and slammed her hand on the button. 'Take me back! Please, take me back!' Terrified the driver wouldn't understand her she scrambled for the words in Italian but the only ones she could find were, *'Portami a casa!'*

*Take me home.*

The driver must have caught the hysteria in her voice for he brought the car to a stop with a screech. In seconds, to a blast of furious horns, he'd performed a U-turn and then they were flying back in the opposite direction on the roads they'd just travelled. No matter how fast he drove though, it wasn't fast enough for Rebecca. Her agitation got too much when they were back at the electric gate and waiting for them to open. Flinging the car door open, she jumped out. Catching the press off guard, she elbowed her way through them, squeezed her way through the small gap that had appeared in the gate, and then ran over the gravel driveway to the front door.

She shoved the door open and raced inside. 'Enzo!' When he didn't immediately answer, she ran into the living room, shouting his name again. 'Enzo!'

The room was empty but the French doors were ajar.

Tears pouring like a waterfall down her face, she sprinted across the room and dived out into the garden. Craning her neck in all directions, she sucked in all the air she could and then screamed his name. *'Enzo!'*

Far in the distance, past the swimming pool and tennis court, a shadow appeared.

Rebecca didn't hesitate. Arms and legs pumping, running faster than she'd ever run in her life, her heart pounding with exertion, tears almost blinding her, she hurtled herself to the statue-like figure and then, before she could even think of what she was doing, leapt at him.

If not for Enzo's innate strength she would have sent them both sprawling. Instead, he caught her, and when her arms flew around his neck and her legs wrapped around his waist, strong hands gripped her tightly to him. Sobbing incoherently, she only realised he'd carried her to the egg seat when he'd sat them both on it.

Straddled over his lap, she disentangled her arms, unburrowed her face from his neck and gazed into bloodshot eyes that were staring at her with complete disbelief.

'Either I did drink too much or this really is you,' he muttered shakily.

'I'm sorry,' she whispered. 'So sorry.'

His lips pulled together and, a sheen appearing in his eyes, he shook his head. 'Don't. You're here. That is enough.'

She caught his hand with both of her own and pressed it against her chest, right in the place her swollen heart was thumping. 'I love you.'

His chest rose. His throat moved as he swallowed. 'And I love you. More than anything.'

'I know.'

His eyes narrowed searchingly. 'Do you?'

Still keeping his hand tight against her chest with one hand, she brushed his cheek with the other. The usually smooth skin prickled with thick, dark stubble.

'You've proved it in so many ways…' Her throat caught as she remembered the teabags she'd found in the cupboard that morning. So many little things. They meant more than all the big things put together. 'What you did was… Well, you know what it was.'

Pain spasmed over his haggard face. 'Unconscionable.'

She squeezed his hand. 'Yes. And I want to blame you for making the last five months one big lie but that's not fair. Some of the blame is on me too.'

His head jerked vehemently. 'None of this is on you. None of it. It is all me.'

'Don't be so egotistical.'

Now his head jerked with surprise.

The pain that had come close to crippling her was abating at the rate of knots, her lungs opening to allow her to breathe. Smiling, she rubbed the back of her fingers over his stubble. 'We were both frightened, Enzo. You called it right when you blamed my insecurities for making me doubt your love but there were other factors at play too. I had doubts from the beginning. Some of that was insecurity but some of it was because you were just *too* perfect. This gorgeous, charming, generous, rich man was pursing me and he was perfect. Honestly, you were so perfect Zeus would have admitted you on Mount Olympus.'

His forehead crinkled and he croaked a laugh. 'Have you not read what those gods got up to?'

She sniggered. Oh, Zeus, but laughter felt good. Wonderful. 'You were perfect and that frightened me because it was a perfection I could never live up to.'

'You are perfect for me.'

She pressed a finger to his lips. 'Shh. Let me speak. Let me get this out and then you can tell me how perfect I am for you.'

His dimples appeared and her heart almost smashed its way out of her. She hadn't realised how desperately she'd been longing to see his dimples again.

'You hid your early years from me because you didn't want me to think you anything less than perfect but I opened up to you about everything, and learning what you'd hidden hurt me until I realised I hadn't bared my soul to you. Not as much as I thought I had. I held things back too, not deliberately, but because I hardly understood them. You did.'

'You mean your parents?'

She nodded. 'I wish you could've met them.'

'I wish I could have met them too.'

She squeezed his fingers. 'They would have adored you. My dad would probably have fallen into a faint if he'd seen your car collection. They really were happy together. I would see my aunts and uncles, and my friends' parents and none of them acted like my parents did, you know, things like squeezing each other's bums when walking past each other and dancing in the kitchen together when a song they both liked came on the radio. That kind of thing.' She sighed. 'I know they loved me. They did. We were a close-knit family but…' She swallowed away the feeling of disloyalty rising up her throat and whispered. 'Sometimes I wanted them to dance with me too.'

He smoothed a lock of her hair. 'I doubt they meant to exclude you.'

'I don't think they even realised they were doing it, but I suppose that feeling of being second best has been in me for so long that I didn't even realise it was there, and that is what I'm trying to explain to you, that there is no way I would have even tried to explain my feelings about it to you, not even two days ago, because deep down I was terrified it would make you look differently at me. You were so ruddy perfect that I kept waiting for the day you realised you were settling for second best and that you could do better than me.'

His nostrils flared with anger, head shaking violently. 'Never.'

'If I'd known about your early years and what an evil witch your mother is, it would have humanised you, because, Enzo, you weren't human. You were the perfect specimen of man, in looks, temperament and good deeds. Even the way you proposed to me, it was just *perfect*, and then there was your superhuman control when I would be begging you to make love to me. Well guess what? I'm glad you have feet of clay. I'm glad that you're as capable of feeling anger and having irrational thoughts and stupid ideas as the rest of us mortals. Most of all, I'm glad that you're mine.'

He pulled his hand out of her hold to cup her cheeks and bring the tip of his nose to hers. 'I will always be yours, Rebecca. Always.'

'I know you will,' she whispered. 'And I will always be yours.'

Their lips fused. Dizzying heat and incredulous wonder filled her. 'Marry me,' she said into his mouth.

Enzo pulled back just enough to stare into her eyes, that searching expression stark in his. His fingers threaded through her hair. 'You are sure?'

'I've never been more sure of anything.

Let's marry as soon as it can be arranged. Just you and me.'

Slowly, the same wonder filling Rebecca appeared as a shine in his eyes. And then his dimples flashed. And his mouth crushed hers.

The sun had long gone to bed before they went back into the villa.

# EPILOGUE

'Do you, Enzo Alessandro Beresi, take Rebecca Emily Folcy to be your wife? To have and to hold from this day forward, for better, for worse, for richer, for poorer, in sickness and in health until death do you part?'

Enzo's clear brown eyes didn't leave Rebecca's face. 'I do.'

Their interlocked fingers squeezed.

'And do you, Rebecca Emily Foley, take Enzo Alessandro Beresi to be your husband? To have and to hold from this day forward, for better, for worse, in—?'

Unable to follow the Italian words for excitement, Rebecca's promise zoomed off her tongue, interrupting the priest in his full flow. 'I do!'

Even the priest laughed. If there had been a congregation watching them, they no doubt would have laughed too, but the only four people invited to witness their marriage were Rebecca's aunt and uncle and Enzo's paternal grandparents. No one else was wanted or needed.

The tiny chapel in the tiny Tuscan village that they were marrying in was a world away from the famous cathedral Rebecca had jilted Enzo at the altar of, and she adored the intimate simplicity of it. Adored that it stripped back all the façade and made it only about the pledging of their lives together. Because that was all that mattered. Their love and commitment to each other. Even their clothing had been stripped of all the pomp and ceremony of their original wedding day, Rebecca's white dress a flowing, bohemian creation, her hair loose, her posy a bunch of sunflowers, Enzo's wedding suit much less formal too, although as snazzy and dapper as the clothes he always wore.

Feeling the weight of the gold ring slide over her finger made Rebecca's heart swell, and when she slid Enzo's ring onto his much larger finger, the expression dancing from his eyes turned the swelling into a balloon bursting to escape the confines of her ribs.

*I love you*, he mouthed.

The happiness infusing her just too much

to contain, she flung her arms around Enzo's neck and kissed him. With more laughter echoing around them, he kissed her back with such enthusiasm her feet were lifted from the ground.

Once all the official stuff was done and they were husband and wife legally and under the sight of God, they left the chapel to find a crowd of local well-wishers had gathered. In the distance, a lone paparazzo was beetling his way up the hill towards them. Considering the lengths Enzo had gone to ensure this wedding was as secret as humanly possible, Rebecca had to admire the pap's tenacity. At her insistence, Rebecca and Enzo had released a short statement which blamed a severe dose of nerves on Rebecca's failure to go ahead with the original wedding—she would tell a thousand lies if it saved Enzo from further humiliation—and ended with their intention to notify people of the rearranged wedding date as soon as possible. All that had been ten days ago, and, despite the press continuing to follow and report on their every move, they were now properly married and other than this one lone paparazzo, they'd got away with the intimacy and privacy they'd craved.

Flinging her arms back around Enzo's neck, she gave the pap his shot. After all, he'd earned it.

*Five years later*

Three-year-old Lily was the first to spot her grandmother's arrival. Practically throwing herself out of the garden playhouse that was almost the same size as the home Rebecca had grown up in, she tore across the lawn to throw herself into her grandmother's arms, squealing, 'Nonna!'

Rebecca and Enzo exchanged their usual bemused 'is this really happening?' looks and watched as the immaculately made-up Robina happily allowed her granddaughter to drag her off to play. She'd arrived for the wedding anniversary party five hours early to look after Lily while Rebecca and Enzo supervised the preparations. Why she'd thought it a good idea to wear a tight-fitting white couture dress for a playdate with a tiny child was anyone's guess, but that was Robina for you.

The rapprochement with her had come about in the days after Lily's birth when Rebecca's sadness that her parents would never meet their first grandchild had tinged the piercing joy of her precious baby. Her daughter only had one surviving grandparent and it had suddenly felt incredibly cruel that she was destined to never meet her. She wouldn't say Lily's birth had softened Enzo when it came to his mother, but he'd agreed to try to put the past behind them and let her back into their lives.

In a move that no one had seen coming, least of all Robina, Lily had taken to her *nonna* right from the start, as content in her arms as she was in her parents'. Bestowing Robina with her very first smile that wasn't wind had resulted in the selfish, narcissistic, morally corrupt retired jewellery thief falling head over heels in love with her granddaughter in return. Watching the couture-dressed and immaculately coiffured Italian woman crawl around on the floor chasing a toddler was something that never grew old, and though Rebecca knew Enzo still struggled to forgive and would never be able to forget, even he accepted that his daughter had enacted a fundamental change in his mother.

With Lily taken care of and their hardworking staff and the army of unobtrusive caterers they'd hired steadily turning the grounds and swimming pool area into an enchanted fairy-tale setting, Rebecca was more than happy to slope off with Enzo for a quick bout of gentle lovemaking; eight months pregnant with their second precious child, it had to be gentle.

She could scarcely believe five years had passed since they'd made their vows. They'd been the happiest years of her life, and they never failed to mark the occasion. Usually they kept their celebrations private but this year had decided to finally throw the big party they'd never got round to having after their secret nuptials.

Later that evening, with the party in full swing and Lily half asleep on Robina's lap, she was glad they'd done it, delighted too that so many of her family and friends had flown over from the UK for it and that none of them were the slightest bit daunted at the company they found themselves partying with. She couldn't stop herself giggling to watch a member of the old Greek royal family flirt manically with one of her cousins: the aristocrat and the hairdresser, ha!

'What are you laughing at?' a deep, velvet voice whispered behind her ear.

She tilted her head and grinned, but before

she could explain, the DJ put on a song that made her heart skip a beat—it was 'their' song.

Enzo held his hand out to her.

Threading her fingers through his, Rebecca gladly let him help her to her feet then heaved her hugely pregnant body onto the specially created dance floor and wrapped her arms around the neck of the man who'd never given her cause to regret marrying him.

'I love you,' she murmured, rising onto her toes to brush a kiss to his lips.

'*Mi amore*,' he breathed into her mouth, filling her with the delicious sensation that time seemed to be in no trouble to lessen.

From the corner of her eye she saw Lily's eyes were wide open, her thumb in her mouth, staring at them with a wistful look.

Unwinding an arm from Enzo's neck, she beckoned their daughter to them. Lily didn't need beckoning twice. Jumping off Robina's lap, she raced onto the dance floor and linked hands with her mummy and daddy. The three of them danced together until Lily's little feet could dance no more.

\* \* \* \* \*